FARTHEST SOUTH
AND OTHER STORIES

PRAISE FOR *FARTHEST SOUTH*

"*Farthest South* makes me want to renew my vows to the short story form. Ethan Rutherford pulls off what other writers can't. His stories are dreamy and crisp. They lull and then startle. Best of all, they don't go anywhere I expect them to. I am obsessed."
—DIANE COOK, author of *The New Wilderness*

"Ethan Rutherford is one of our great artists of catastrophe. Drawing on landscapes both mythic—the fairy tale, the ghost story—and domestic, this collection illuminates terrors that feel at once prescient and eternal. *Farthest South* is a masterpiece."
—LAURA VAN DEN BERG, author of *I Hold a Wolf by the Ears*

"In these disquieting stories, the surface of seemingly placid, ordinary American life gives way to startling eruptions of the strange, the marvelous, and the dreadful. Each story is an uncanny revelation, as if Nathaniel Hawthorne had decided to take up residence among us. 'What did I miss?' numerous characters ask in the collection, and while the characters often do not know, Ethan Rutherford does. A brilliant and literally wonderful collection."
—RATTAWUT LAPCHAROENSAP, author of *Sightseeing*

"Again and again you can feel the stories in *Farthest South* striking out after fascination and surprising themselves with wisdom. Ethan Rutherford pairs a classic style with a haunted vision. Narratives that are all grace and ease at the beginning gradually become soaked in dread and hallucination. Reading them is by equal measures comforting and jolting, like sinking into a warm bath and feeling the brush of something living against your body."
—KEVIN BROCKMEIER, author of *The Ghost Variations*

"Ethan Rutherford's stories combine nail-biting tension with crystalline description, humor, and endings that are as marvelously strange as they are rewarding. Toggling between the eerie and the radiantly familiar, *Farthest South* is unsettling in all the best ways. This is a beautifully spellbinding book."
—JULIE SCHUMACHER, author of
   Dear Committee Members

"The nine gorgeous and disorienting tales in *Farthest South* explore the terrors of love and attachment. The characters stumble through a contemporary reality they cannot decipher, guided by the unsound logic of dreams. Rutherford's imagination is vast, as is his compassion for our lostness. These are sublime, disquieting, and consequential stories for our moment."
—AMITY GAIGE, author of *Sea Wife*

"Stories that test the boundaries of the fictional imagination."
—*KIRKUS*, starred review

FARTHEST SOUTH

SOUTH

AND OTHER STORIES

ETHAN RUTHERFORD

DEEP
VELLUM

Dallas, Texas

A
STRANGE
OBJECT

Austin, Texas

DEEP VELLUM   A STRANGE OBJECT

The stories in this collection have appeared in slightly different forms in the following publications:

"Ghost Story" in *Tin House*, "The Baby" in *Post Road*, "Farthest South" in *BOMB*, "The Diver" (as "The Soul Collector") in *Conjunctions*.

Published by
A Strange Object, an imprint of Deep Vellum
© 2021 Ethan Rutherford. All rights reserved.

LIBRARY OF CONGRESS CATALOGING-IN-PUBLICATION DATA
Names: Rutherford, Ethan, author.
Title: Farthest south and other stories / Ethan Rutherford.
Description: Dallas, Texas : Deep Vellum Publishing ; Austin, Texas :
    A Strange Object, [2021]
Identifiers: LCCN 2020044988 (print) | LCCN 2020044989 (ebook) |
    ISBN 9781646050475 (trade paperback) | ISBN 9781646050482
    (ebook)
Subjects: LCGFT: Short stories.
Classification: LCC PS3618.U7785 F37 2021 (print) | LCC PS3618.U7785
    (ebook) | DDC 813/.6—dc23
LC record available at https://lccn.loc.gov/2020044988
LC ebook record available at https://lccn.loc.gov/2020044989

This is a work of fiction. Any resemblances to actual persons, living or dead, events, or locales are coincidental.

Cover design by Nayon Cho
Book design by Amber Morena
Illustrations by Anders Nilsen

For Rusty and Paul

CONTENTS

Oh golden dreams
Golden dreams all lose their glow
I don't need perfection, I love the whole
Oh give me a life that needs correction
Nobody loves, loves perfection
Loneliness, loneliness will run you through
All the kids are laughing, I'm laughing too.
—HAMILTON LEITHAUSER

Dorothy changed direction on the way to the main road.
She drove back to town and then went on to the museum
gardens, parked the car and walked around, looking at
the trees and flowers. There were two old women being
pushed in wheelchairs by uniformed nurses. Me, one
day, she thought. And between now and then, nothing
that can be done to avoid it, except an early death. But
the gardens were pleasant.
—RACHEL INGALLS, *Mrs. Caliban*

FARTHEST SOUTH
AND OTHER STORIES

GHOST STORY
\\\\\\\\\\

SOREN LIVED WITH HIS WIFE on the fourteenth floor
of an apartment complex in the middle of the city. When
they were younger, this apartment had suited them well—
it was full of single people, and everyone liked to stay
up late around the rooftop pool to watch the lights of the
neighboring buildings—but now they had two children,
and the apartment had begun to feel small. Hana, his wife,
was eager to move, but what could they do? They could
barely afford the place they had. Some nights, after they
made love or finished reading, Hana would quiz him on
his top requirement for their new apartment, as if talking about it would make it real. Usually Soren would say

wraparound deck, or *large fireplace*, but what he really wanted was a house by the sea with a view of a lighthouse, where he could hear its low warning wash over the waves. Hana's top requirement was always a pool of her own. She went swimming every day as soon as Soren got home from work, but the pool at their apartment was often crowded and not ideal for swimmers. It's for jumping, Hana would say a little sadly.

Soren's job was, as he put it to anyone who asked, too boring to explain. He worked in advertising and was part of a large team that tried to convince celebrities to use their clients' products. It had been exciting at first, but the hours were long, and he spent the majority of his time in front of the computer; and since he was the new guy, most days he had to be in early and stay late. This meant that the only time he saw his children during the week was for breakfast or after dinner, right before they were about to go to sleep. It was not ideal, but it was better than his father had done. They had the weekends, but those had a way of evaporating as well: the older boy spent time with his friends now that he was in a new school and had just entered first grade; the younger one had a schedule full of playdates. Hana liked the other parents and was good at small talk, but these playdates were awkward for Soren, so he usually skipped them to do the grocery shopping for the week. He walked the aisles with headphones on, whistling. It was the only time he got to be alone.

Tonight, he had been kept at work by a client who was wondering about the best way to get the moisturizer his company produced "onto the hands" of a famous soap-opera villain. Soren listened until he could listen no more, and then he said he would have to think on it and call the client back first thing in the morning.

Hana was waiting for him in the kitchen. "They're ready for you," she said in an irritated voice. She was already dressed in her bathing suit and cap. Soren knew from experience that this meant that she'd had a hard night with the boys.

"What happened?" he asked.

"Oh," she said, "the usual."

Soren liked seeing her in her bathing suit, and the incongruity of her standing in the middle of their apartment half-naked and fretting about her goggles and nose plug gave him the beginning of an erection. They were still very much in love. Hana claimed she didn't mind his soft belly, liked it even, but it made him self-conscious, so he rarely swam anymore.

"They want a ghost story," Hana told him. "They said to make it scary."

"What should I tell them?" Soren said.

Hana shrugged. "I don't know," she said. "How about the one about the seal lady?"

Soren hadn't thought about that story in a long time. He wasn't so sure he was looking forward to remembering it.

"That's a really scary story," he said.

Hana picked up her towel. "Then tell them something else," she said. "What do I care? I'm going to go swim with a bunch of young adults who don't know what work is."

Soren had the feeling that perhaps the night had gone even worse than he'd suspected. Hana worked full-time too, but she'd made a deal with her boss that she could pick up the children from school at 4:30 pm every day. So she would do that, feed the kids, get them ready for bed, and then Soren would come home and tell them a story. It wasn't a fair arrangement.

"Did you guys give Mom trouble tonight?" he asked his children when he opened the door to their room. They had bunk beds, but they couldn't agree on who got top and who got bottom, so the beds were just two singles next to each other with almost no space in between.

"No," they said.

Soren knew they weren't telling the truth, but he didn't mind. He was about to tell them a scary story, but he had to remember the details first. He sat on the older one's bed and made himself comfortable. He noticed they'd dressed in matching pajamas, and the younger one had a decorative Band-Aid on his nose. This was generally the best part of his day.

"When I was little," he began. It was going to be a Young Soro story. The children were excited.

THE YOUNG SORO STORIES he told were often stories from his childhood. When he could, he added a moral or a lesson or at least a piece of wisdom to the story. For example, he had quit music lessons when he was younger because his piano teacher had tried too early to teach him jazz. That was a deep regret. So to make up for it he tried to invent a story about a boy who stuck to music and lived a more enriched life. Most of the stories were about friendship and the importance of having a brother. If he was being honest with himself, some of the details in the Young Soro stories were ripped off from the children's book series Frog and Toad—but there was no real harm in that. He remembered what he could, and tried to stick to the happy stuff. More than once he'd inadvertently included product placement—Young Soro wanting nothing more than, say, a Pepsi—and he was appalled at this slipup. He was good at his job, but if he was honest, his job also repulsed him, and made him think badly of the people who bought his clients' products.

All the Young Soro stories began in Vancouver, British Columbia, and Soren was pleased, now that he no longer lived in that beautiful city, to return to those secret corners of his memory. There he could visit his mother and father, who was long dead. There he could make mischief in the corridors that linked his old classrooms. He found, as he told these stories, that occasionally he would go into a sort of trance, not unpleasant, but the boys would gently rock him if he went on too long or if he stopped talking altogether. Then he would say, "Ah, where were we?" and they would remind him. There were different layers to each Young Soro story, and Soren was usually aware that the stories were more like a series of locked doors than anything else. His children heard one thing, and he heard, as he talked, another. The stories often got away from him, and if that happened, he would nervously search for a way to wrap them up in a satisfying manner. But if you didn't know the ending, it was always possible to say: "To be continued."

"This is a very scary story," Soren said now. He'd interrupted his own story before it had really even begun. "Are you sure you want to hear it?"

"Of course," the boys said. They huddled closer together. It was just beginning to get dark outside.

"Okay," Soren said. "Just stop me if you get scared, all right?" The children nodded, and he began again.

I WAS LITTLE when my parents divorced. It was not a happy parting, but I was too young to remember the particulars except that my mother cried a lot for a while and then one day she just stopped. My father moved to Anchorage when I was seven years old because he was a ship captain, and he fished for salmon in the summer. He never wrote and rarely called, but for my twelfth birthday he invited me to spend the summer with him in Alaska, and part of that would mean that I'd get to be with him on his boat. She was a small fishing boat, named *Josephine*, after his favorite singer. He had a crew of three men who would go out on the water with him during salmon season, and they would make enough money to work part-time for the rest of the year.

My mother was nervous about this arrangement, but eventually relented. My older sister had been in trouble at school, and my mother needed the summer to sort her out. In some ways, having me away from the house would be the best thing for everyone.

I'd been to Anchorage before, but never for such a long time. And I was excited to fish. I was very firmly in a worship-my-father stage of my life. I realize now that much of that probably had to do with the fact that he was gone and I got to imagine the father he might be. When he picked me up at the small airport, he looked shorter than I remembered, and also heavier around the middle. There was a young woman beside him who was shy about introducing herself, but I knew right away that she was his girlfriend. Don't tell your mom, he said. Yes, please don't, said the woman.

My father's house was not too far from the docks where the fishing boats tied up. I'd arrived early for the season and thought maybe I could assist him with the nets, but after the first day it was clear I wasn't going to be much help. My father was kind about it—he had other guys working with him on the sewing and the laying out.

THE SMALLER BOY SHIFTED under his covers. The older one sighed. They didn't want to hear about salmon fishing. Taking inventory of the different nets had actually been Soren's favorite part of that summer, but he knew he should skip ahead. *I'm taking too long to get to the Seal Lady*, Soren thought. And he was right about that.

ANYWAY, I HAD A LOT OF TIME on my hands. My father's new girlfriend was always at the house, and she made me uncomfortable when my father wasn't there—sometimes she would talk loudly on the phone to someone about me, other times she'd walk around in her underwear and ignore me completely—so I spent most of my time outside, exploring the town. Where my father lived was pretty far out there. There was a main street, where you could get all your fishing supplies, and then a 7-Eleven with a *Street Fighter II* arcade game that was always fritzing out, and about six different bars that I never went into even though they let kids in. But as soon as you left this main street, the roads branched off into deep, dark woods. Huge old trees. Black shadows. Smelly dirt. I would go for long walks in these woods—sometimes following trails, and sometimes making my own. I never ran into anyone else, though there were a number of abandoned houses scattered throughout the thick trunks and growth of the forest. They looked like old, weather-beaten faces that had collapsed in on themselves. All the windows cracked or gone, taken over by blackberry bushes. I walked into a few of these grimy houses, but always left quickly. I was worried that someone would catch me there, and tell my father, and I'd get sent home. I was trying extra hard to be a good son, someone he would be proud of.

Each day, I would walk for hours. My dad just let me wander while he got the boat ready. He never had any idea where I was. When it was time for dinner he would stand at the back door and whistle loudly with his fingers, and I would hear it and come back. Simple.

On the night before we were heading out on the boat, my father and his girlfriend got into a huge fight. He'd spent all day at the docks, and missed dinner, which was now cold. It didn't seem like such a big deal, but she stomped around the kitchen, and at some point began throwing dishes on the ground. My father looked ashamed and asked me if I wouldn't mind walking around for a little while so they could sort this out. It made me angry, but of course I said okay.

I left the house with no direction in mind. I kept my head down while I was walking, and once I was in the woods, I found a stick the size of a baseball bat and began hitting bushes as I tromped around. When I got tired of doing that and looked up, I realized I was in a part of the woods that was unfamiliar to me. The trees, I noticed, were larger here, and sort of a black and ash color. They were huge and beautiful. It wasn't too dark, but my throat tightened a bit. I knew that the water was south, and if I could find the water, I could find my way back to my dad's house, so I set off in the direction that seemed the most south.

After about ten minutes, the path opened and I came upon a house I'd never seen before. This house belonged to the Seal Lady, but I didn't know it at the time—it stood like all the other houses I'd seen in the woods, though in slightly better condition, and it was clear that someone lived there. Thinking I could perhaps get directions back to the docks, I knocked on the door. No one answered; when I knocked again, the door swung halfway open. I don't know why, but when I called and got no response, I pushed the door all the way open and stepped inside.

I hadn't eaten since breakfast. My head had begun to ache, and as my stomach turned, I suddenly became aware of how hungry I was. I knew it wasn't right to steal, but I was lost; and since no one was home, I thought maybe I'd just see if there were some chips or something—a piece of food that wouldn't be easily missed, or a handful of nuts—and then I'd be on my way.

The house smelled like a mothy old sweater; the curtains were drawn. The filthy carpet was unusually soft and springy. I did not aim to linger. But as I snuck across the sparsely furnished living room, my attention caught on a glass case set against the back wall. It was clean and well-lit, and as I got closer, I saw that it held a number of porcelain figurines. They were small—none larger than the size, say, of an index finger—but they were arranged in an arresting way: all the figures stood in a circle, as if staring at one another. In the middle of the circle was an odd-looking golden fish: it had a salmon's hook-nosed head and the long body of an eel.

I should've shrugged and gone on to the kitchen, but I was drawn to the case; and as I examined the figurines more closely, I was surprised to discover that their faces were the same, and that each, to an alarming degree, looked exactly like my father's girlfriend. Without thinking, I opened the thin glass doors and picked one up. I hadn't been mistaken: up close, the features were hers. The figurine was heavier than I expected and seemed well made; but as I turned it in my hand, her head fell off and landed on the carpet between my feet without a sound. *That's not good*, I remember thinking, but I didn't reach down to pick it up. Instead, I squeezed what remained of the figurine in my hand, and her arms broke off like small, dry twigs. Something moved inside me, some dark feeling, and I grabbed and angrily crushed each of the little figu-

rines—one wore a blue robe, one was dressed as a fisher-woman, one was a nurse, one wore an old-fashioned bathing suit. It was satisfying to destroy these brittle, small dolls. I was thorough and methodical. I felt powerful, even though I knew it wouldn't change anything.

I heard a sound behind me then—and when I turned, I saw that the Seal Lady had appeared and was standing in the foyer of her strange and decrepit home. I know now that she is somewhat famous in those parts—you say "Seal Lady" and everyone knows whom you mean and has stories about her—but at the time I'd never heard of her. As for why she's called Seal Lady, it's pretty simple—for some reason that is hard to put into words, she reminds everyone who sees her of a big and dangerous leopard seal. She's a half seal, half woman. But you never *catch* her looking like a seal. That's just the impression she gives. You know, when you are talking to her, that you are talking to something not completely human, but something older, and when you think back on your conversation you think: *Those are the darkest eyes I've ever seen. I've just spoken to a seal.*

"DID SHE HAVE TEETH?" one of the boys asked Soren.

"Yes, she did," he answered. "Long and yellow and razor sharp. You couldn't miss them."

"Did she say she was going to eat you up?" the other boy asked.

"She did," Soren said. He paused, as if he wasn't sure he wanted to go on. "But then she said there was a way that she wouldn't eat me up."

"How?" the boy said.

"Be patient," Soren said. "I'm getting to that part."

I WAS SCARED out of my mind. She was unbelievably imposing. Though she was hunched over like a regular old person, her head still brushed the ceiling, and it felt as though the house had shrunk around her. She said she recognized me as my father's son, and that she knew I wasn't from the area, so perhaps I hadn't heard of her. She said she had great power and would demonstrate that to me now so that I would pay attention to what she said next.

At this her eyes flashed a little, but there wasn't anything earthshaking going on. I was beginning to think maybe I could make a run for it. The only thing was that when I tried to run, I found that I could not, since the carpet held my boots.

Think of a secret you haven't told anyone, and I will guess it, she said. And when I speak it back to you, you'll know that I'm powerful and can read your thoughts.

I didn't want to think of any secret, so I thought of a long series of numbers instead. I repeated these numbers in my head until they were all I could hear, and I could see the integers scrolling away from me into the distance like little flapping birds.

Of course, she told me the exact numbers, even with decimal points. And then she laughed, because she'd been expecting a secret.

Now, let me show you something, she said, and her jaw unhinged like a snake's. Her head split almost in half, and I saw rows and rows of jagged brown teeth. Impressive, right? she said. She walked closer and stood so near that I could smell her salty musk. Those figurines, she said, were the only thing I loved on this earth. They were invaluable to me, and you have broken them as if they meant nothing at all.

I apologized profusely, but she didn't seem to care. I could feel her hot breath on my neck. She stank of rotting kelp. I thought for sure I was dead. I closed my eyes and braced myself, but when nothing happened, I opened them and saw that the Seal Lady was sitting in one of her ratty chairs near the fireplace.

This is a situation, she said, that needs to be made right. You are in debt to me. And by rights, I am now allowed to destroy something that *you* hold dear. She closed her eyes as if in deep thought and stayed that way for a long time. I thought perhaps she'd fallen asleep, but I knew I wouldn't be so lucky. Here's the arrangement, she finally said. Her eyes were still closed. Either I can tie you up here and eat your fingers and toes one by one until they are gone—at which point I will slowly season and eat the rest of you, call my cubs, and scatter your bones into the sea—and *then* I will find something you hold dear and destroy it, or else you can work to repay your debt.

I was so frightened that for a minute or two I couldn't speak. Eventually, I managed a nod to signal I would do my best.

This pleased her, I think. Here is what will happen, she said. When you are fishing with your father, every now and then you will pull a golden fish from the ocean. This fish will come only to your boat, and only you will be able to discern its true color. When you find this fish, you must eat every part of it. Only by eating the entire fish will you stay true to our agreement. You will receive between five and seven fish, and each one carries in its stomach something I am looking for. When you have completed your fishing expedition, bring me the contents of each fish's stomach, and you will be released from your debt.

I nodded again. When I looked down, I noticed I had wet myself. There, there, she said. She handed me some napkins. Just stick to our agreement, and keep it to yourself, and everything will be fine. I know your father's boat—I know all the boats around here—and I will be watching and waiting for you. And with a craggy hand, she motioned for me to leave.

Somehow, I found my way back to my father's house. He was cleaning up in the kitchen. I wanted to tell him what had happened, but every time I thought about doing so, I imagined the Seal Lady, and couldn't say a thing.

I stepped on some glass he'd missed on the kitchen floor. I'm sorry, he said. That wasn't about you. She just gets like this before I go on any sort of trip.

"AND THE WEIRD PART," Soren told the boys, "was that even though it felt as if I'd been gone for hours, by the clock I had been gone only fifteen minutes."

"That's not the weird part, Dad," one of them said.

"You're right," Soren said. "This Young Soro story is getting away from me."

"I'm going to get some water," the older boy said.

"That's fine," said Soren, and moved a little so that his son could get out from under the covers.

While his son was gone, Soren tried to remember if he had left out any important details. He couldn't think of any, though he had changed two small things. The first was that of course the fight, to some degree, had been about him. His father had either forgotten or neglected to tell his girlfriend that Soren was coming until they were on the way to pick him up, and she was understandably upset about that. And the second was that instead of a complicated series of numbers, he had, in fact, thought of a secret, and it was one that the Seal Lady had guessed right away. The secret was this: his older sister was no longer a virgin, and everyone at school knew about it. That was why she'd had a hard time that summer. That wasn't a detail he felt bad about changing, though. It might've derailed the story.

The boy came back with a full glass of water.

"If she was a seal," the boy said, "how did she walk?"

Soren thought for a minute. "It was more like just her head was a seal's," he finally said. "She had big arms and legs. It's hard to remember. She was horrible to look at."

"Oh," the boy said.

"Okay," Soren said. "Let's get back to it."

THE *JOSEPHINE* WAS a medium-sized fishing boat, but her cabin was small. On board it was me, my dad, and a crew of three other guys. My job was to help the crew with the haul, and sometimes I served as a messenger between the deck and the wheelhouse, where my dad spent most of his time. I tried to be as useful as possible, and in my mind, I was essential to the successful operation of the *Josephine*, but I know now that for the most part everyone was barely tolerating me.

My dad had bought me a whole set of foul-weather gear—boots, overalls, outer jacket, fleece, hat, and insulated gloves. I knew it was expensive. It made me happy that he had taken the time to pick all my gear out, and that he'd chosen the same colors for me as he wore. The other guys on the ship all had yellow gear, head to foot. But we had orange stuff.

It took us about a day to get to the fishing grounds. The farther we got from the marina, the less I thought about the Seal Lady. Fishing is a hard job, and I had a lot to learn. The sea was calm and looked solid and flat near the horizon, but still I got seasick the first day and spent most of the afternoon staring out over the bow, trying to keep my attention on the shore some five miles away.

The way fishing on the *Josephine* worked was pretty standard: you set the net out in the water with a skiff and waited a few hours; then a motorized winch reeled the net back in and hoisted the catch over the deck. After the net disgorged its fish—and each haul could be hundreds of stunned and flopping salmon—you packed them into the refrigerated hold, where they stayed until you took them to a weigh station. I was too young to pilot the skiff by myself and wasn't allowed to operate the winch. Most days I sat with my dad in the wheelhouse and then scampered down to help with the packing once the fish were dropped on deck.

What I hadn't really counted on, though, was how slow it could be out on the water. You'd set the net and wait, wait, wait. Then you'd reel it in, putter to a different part of the bay, and do it again. My dad didn't let us listen to the radio unless the net was down, and even then I could never find a station I liked. It was always just classic rock from the seventies up and down the dial. And then, after a while, my dad would signal that it was enough and he'd flip over to AM to listen to the tide and weather report, which was read by a guy who sounded exactly like a bored robot. I imagined him in a lighthouse somewhere, mumbling into a small microphone with the patience of an old machine.

My father chain-smoked as he watched the swell, trying to guess where the fish would be next. We didn't talk very much—he didn't ask me about school, and he was hesitant to start a conversation, as if he was worried he might say or ask the wrong thing—but that was okay with me. He didn't say anything to me about his girlfriend, and he didn't ask about my mother. But I was happy. I loved being on that boat. I felt as if I was being treated like a man for the first time in my life. It had everything to do with silence.

For the first two weeks or so, we had pretty bad luck. The hauls were small, and everyone was in a lousy mood. But soon there was a storm that came up from the west. It was the first time I was frightened aboard the *Josephine*— the waves were large and broke in the wind, tossed us around. My dad made me go below, and I stayed there, listening to the engine sort of sputter and puff as we went up the side of one wave and down the other. Finally, it was over. Everyone was a little green, and very much relieved. And then, as we set the net and pulled our first haul of the day, we saw that the storm's churn had filled the bay with confused and angry salmon.

"AND IT WAS THEN," Soren said dramatically, "that I saw the first golden fish."

"Did you eat it?" the older boy said.

"Of course!" Soren said. "I was terrified!"

"What did it taste like?" the boy said.

Soren thought for a minute. "It was the most repulsive thing I've ever eaten," he finally said. "I could barely choke it down." He coughed. "Anyway, in its stomach was a figurine much like the ones I had broken. The difference, though, was that it was naked but had no private parts."

"Weird," said one of the boys.

Soren thought for a minute more. "That's not even the weird part," he said.

THE WEIRD PART WAS that this figurine could move on its own, albeit in a limited way. It was, I think, some sort of tiny automaton. It also looked very much like my father's girlfriend. And if you left her lying down in one place too long, she would slowly rise and walk mechanically around as if she were searching for something. I had eaten this fish down below in the cabin where I slept so no one would see me, and now I was stuck with this walking doll. I found a little box and I put her in it, and then I tied a piece of twine around the box and stowed it under my bunk. I had begun to think that my encounter with the Seal Lady was something I had just invented for some obscure reason, but now I knew how wrong I was.

The next golden fish came a week later on the morning haul. I had to grab it off the deck and shove it into my boot before anyone saw me take it. It squirmed and squirmed as I quickly excused myself and went to the bathroom, where I took it out of my boot and put it on the small counter next to the toilet. It looked just like a regular salmon, no doubt about that, but its scales were streaked with gold and red, and when the light hit the fish's flank it was almost difficult to look at. It was really a beautiful fish. I had hit the first one on the head with a winch handle until it stopped moving, but this one was pretty still, and clapped his gills open and shut on the counter in a sad way until finally he gave a last spasm and died. When I took my first bite, I thought I might pass out. This fish tasted much worse than the previous one. I felt as though I was putting something long dead into my mouth. My stomach got upset, and cold strands of saliva shot from the back of my tongue. I swallowed and had to sit on the toilet for a few minutes before I could take another bite. It took forever, but eventually I choked it down. In its stomach was another small figurine, dripping with digestive juice. I washed it off in the sink and put it in the box with the first one. I didn't watch long enough to see if it moved or not—I was too disgusted— but when I went to sleep that night, I heard a scratching sound coming from the box, and so I assumed it did. The scratching wasn't relentless, and quieted down after a few minutes. I was worried my dad would hear it, but he was dead on his feet—and when he came below to lie on the bunk next to mine, he slept through everything until his alarm went off.

Meanwhile, we were catching a lot of fish. More than we could even keep up with. Our hold kept filling earlier than we expected, and we'd have to go to a processing ship to empty everything out. Each haul was met with laughter and high fives and eager whoops. The crew gave thanks to the sea and started drinking earlier and earlier at night. My dad was as happy as I'd ever seen him. He'd put his hand on my shoulder as each net came in. He introduced me to the guys on the processing ship as his good luck charm. Now and then he'd let me steer the boat and show me how to make tight turns by working the engine's throttle against the wheel.

Sometimes he would let me stay up and we'd talk as we waited for the net to fill. I don't really remember what we talked about—not everything is coming back to me—but I remember he would tell me about his favorite movies, and his favorite books, and I would nod and say, I've read that, or I'll check that out. One night he told me the story about how he and my mother met, which was different from the story she'd told me. He said he was sad that he didn't live closer to us, but he needed to be up in Alaska. I said it was fine with me, even though it wasn't. It just seemed like the right thing to say on that dark and drifting boat.

About a week later, when we were unloading the hold at the processing ship, I saw the third golden fish. I must've missed it when it had come aboard. I reached for it, and almost lost my balance, but finally I plucked it from the mass of other fish as they were being transferred. The guy on the processing ship looked at me as though he couldn't believe someone would let a twelve-year-old run around on a boat like this. I didn't know if he had seen me take the fish or not. I didn't stick around.

This one was inedible. I'd found it late, and it was pretty much jelly at this point, held together by bones. The stench was unmanageable and reminded me of something in the midst of a dark decay. My eyes burned just trying to get close enough to place it in my mouth. I tried cutting it up into smaller pieces, but that only made things more disgusting; I must've punctured an intestine, or

something, because this strange green pus oozed out and ran all over the counter. I couldn't eat this fish. Not this one. I knew I couldn't.

I did some rationalizing. I figured that the Seal Lady couldn't know everything, and that if it had been this easy to miss this particular fish when it first came aboard, why couldn't I say I'd just never seen it at all? I told myself I'd keep a better eye on the catch from now on, and would eat the fish as they came in, when they were fresher. I scooped this fish up and dumped it into a plastic grocery bag. I wiped the counter down with a sponge and put the sponge in the bag too. I could feel sweat forming on my face. Then I took the bag topsides, and when no one was looking, I tipped it over the port rail. I saw now that the fish was mostly liquid, and it leaked into the sea with the thickness of oil. As I poured it out, I thought I might faint; the stench was so unpleasant. One of its flat eyeballs stuck on the bag's handle, and I panicked and waved the bag to shake it loose. Just then, I remembered the figurine—I'd been so disgusted that I'd forgotten to check—but it was too late. It fell out of the bag and hit the water with a loud plop and sank immediately into the calm sea like a hammer.

I must've looked sick, because when he saw me my dad asked what was wrong. I said I just needed to lie down, and that's what I did. From the cabin, I could hear my dad joking with the processing guys. The engine alarm sounded, and then the engine turned and shook the boat to life, and we were heading back out into the bay.

That night we anchored, which was rare. While I stayed in the cabin, my dad and the rest of the crew celebrated how well the summer was going; they dug into the cooler, found some seventies rock on the radio, and drank late into the night. I listened to them talk and laugh, and that ambient sound—the warmth of listening in on a gathering of men talking to one another—took me away from the memory of the fish. I fell asleep without even knowing I was tired.

Later in the night, much later, I think, because everything was so quiet, I woke to a scratching sound from the box under my bed. It took me a while to figure out where I was. My dad was asleep across from me, snoring. I was in my sleeping bag. The boat was rocking on her anchor line. I heard the scratching sound again, and then I was fully awake.

I didn't want to wake my father, so I shook the box once to quiet the figurines. Then I untied the twine and opened the lid. They were intact. They didn't move, but they watched me closely as if they were afraid of what I might do. I shut the box, double knotted the twine, and stowed it back under my bunk with an extra blanket to muffle the sound. Then I realized I still felt a little sick from the fish, my stomach was weightless, and so after making sure no more sound came from the box, I tiptoed out of our cabin, walked past the other sleeping guys, and went topsides to get some air.

The night was black. There was no moon. I could see some distant stars, and I watched as a few came unstuck and frizzled across the sky. The only sound I heard was the waves gently lapping at our hull as we bobbed on our anchor. It's hard to overstate the beauty of a summer night in Alaska.

But then I heard another sound, a soft grunting and splashing, and when I looked to the stern, I saw that some sort of creature was swimming toward the *Josephine* in the perfect dark. I tried to convince myself it was a large otter or a fish, but I knew in my heart it was the Seal Lady. Her stroke was elegant, and with each kick she set off a small constellation of phosphorescence in the water around her. I'd never been so scared in my life. I wanted to wake up my dad, but somehow I knew that would be a bad idea. She made it to the *Josephine*, and then I saw two huge and dripping paws flop over the side and she hoisted herself up and soon stood on deck.

SOREN SUDDENLY STOPPED his story. "May I have a sip of your water?" he asked his son.

"Sure," his son said, and handed him the glass.

"What happened?" the younger boy said. "Did she try to bite you?"

Soren sighed, and set the now-empty glass of water on the bedside table. "No," he said. "Worse."

"Worse?" the older one said.

"She pointed below deck, to where my father was sleeping," Soren said softly, "and told me that the next time she came back, it would be for him."

"And then what happened?" the older one said.

"She just jumped overboard," Soren said. "And sank into the dark water."

"What did you do?" the younger one asked.

"Well," said Soren, "I certainly ate every golden fish I saw. I choked them all down. I've never eaten such wretched food in my life. I couldn't tell anyone. I felt so trapped. It was awful." Soren sighed. "I kept all the figurines in the box under my bed," he said. "By the end of the summer I had six of them."

"Did they all move like the first one?"

"No," Soren said. "That sort of stopped happening."

"Oh," the younger one said. Soren could tell he was disappointed. He didn't know if he wanted to tell this next part or not. "There's one more thing," Soren said. "I forgot to tell you the scary part."

NEAR THE END OF OUR TRIP, we anchored again, and I saw the Seal Lady one more time. Everyone was exceedingly happy about how the catch had gone—this had been a record summer for the *Josephine*, and everyone aboard would be making quite a bit of money. This was not the case with the other fishing boats in the area—in fact, most had turned up almost nothing for their weeks of effort—and so we felt doubly lucky. On our final night on the water, the radio picked up a country station, and we took turns doing Johnny Cash impressions. Then there was a Willie Nelson back-to-back, and when "Whiskey River" came on, my dad let me take a few sips of his beer. Eventually everyone turned in. When I woke up, I knew the Seal Lady was aboard. I looked over at my dad, who was sleeping soundly. His face was so relaxed he appeared about twenty years younger, flush and unwrinkled and as though he had never smoked. For some reason, I reached out and put my hand on his cheek. I didn't want to wake him up, I just wanted to touch him. I realized I'd never touched him, or anyone, like that before.

The Seal Lady was sitting on the stern of the *Josephine*. She wore an elegant blue robe and was singing in a high, lilting voice. In each hand she held a golden fish, and in her dark eyes somehow I could see the carcasses of many others. Someone on this boat is very sad, she said. Yes, yes, maybe it's you. Maybe we're the same. She held up one of the golden fish, slowly lowered it into her mouth, and swallowed it whole. Then she let loose a satisfied belch. No, she said. Nobody wants you. That's your secret. She stood and opened her arms; her robe hung open; she motioned for me to come to her. I was petrified. I couldn't move. Smart, she said, and threw the other fish into the bay. Then, as I watched, she began to rock back and forth, and started to scratch at her long arms as if she had bugs crawling under her skin. At first, she appeared perplexed. Then it seemed as if a ferocious energy was gathering around her. She brought one arm to her mouth and began to gnaw angrily at the flesh at her wrist. I wanted to ask if she was all right, but I didn't; I couldn't make myself talk. Then, with a sharp cry, she unhinged her jaw and bit her hand completely off and swallowed it in one choking gulp.

The entire ocean seemed to still. One day, she finally said, everything you love will be gone from you. And then, just like that, she disappeared.

The next morning, we woke to find that one of the crew members was no longer aboard. We couldn't find him anywhere. We did a quick inventory—he hadn't taken anything—and anyway, where was he going to go? It seemed as though he'd evaporated into thin air. We radioed it into the coast guard, but there wasn't much they could do. No one had seen him fall into the water. He hadn't taken the skiff. We searched for two days. Then we went home.

Later, we heard that when they found his body it was covered with bite marks. He'd washed up on the other side of the bay and been pulled in by a set netter. They said he'd been chewed up pretty badly by a propeller and had probably been hit by at least one or two boats, in addition to being nibbled on by fish.

"AND TO THIS DAY," Soren said, "I can't figure out why she would've attacked him."

"Was he the sad one?" the younger boy asked.

Soren thought for a second and put his fingers to his

chin. "Perhaps," he finally said. "But I can't even remember his name."

He'd lost the thread to his own story, and the boys knew it. At this point in the night they were just asking questions to see how much longer they could stay up.

"Anyway," he said. "As soon as we pulled back into the marina, I hopped off the boat and took the figurines to that old strange house. No one was home, so I left them in their box on the front porch and ran away as fast as I could. And I never saw the Seal Lady again."

Soren stood up and cracked his knuckles. His left foot was asleep from the position it had been in for so long. "Good night," he said, and tucked one boy in, and then the other.

"Good night," they said back.

"I hope you're not too frightened," Soren said when he got to the door.

"No," said the older one.

"Well," said Soren. "You should be more helpful to your mother when you can be, just the same."

"What?" the younger boy said, but Soren had turned out the lights and was already walking down the hall.

HANA HADN'T RETURNED from her swimming, which was strange. Soren checked the time. The story had taken him just over an hour. He'd have to get it down a little better if the Seal Lady was going to be a story he told over and over. He poured himself a drink and sat on the couch facing the window. Across the street in one of the neighboring apartment buildings he saw a man, roughly his age, working out on a treadmill. *Why wouldn't you run outside?* thought Soren, but then he realized he didn't care at all what this man did.

He hadn't told the whole story about what happened with the Seal Lady. To his deep shame, he had never delivered the figurines. He'd tried, but when he'd gone into the woods, he couldn't find the Seal Lady's house, and became very lost. He'd been too afraid to try again, and at the end of the summer, when it came time to return to Vancouver, he took the figurines with him. It was true that they no longer moved when he pulled them from the box, but he found that they had a special meaning for him, just the same. And that strange night on the boat wasn't, in fact, the last time he saw the Seal Lady. When he turned fourteen, she began appearing in his dreams as a younger and more seductive version of herself. The dreams were highly sexual, and embarrassed him a great deal, but he could not control them. Eventually, around the time he went to college, they stopped.

It was during his third year of college that the *Josephine* sank, and his father drowned. At that point in Soren's life, he and his father hadn't spoken in years because of something his father had said to his mother when he announced he was getting remarried. At the funeral, his father's wife wore a long black dress, and would not speak to him. At her side was a young child everyone assumed was hers, but no one knew for sure. Gone for good, his sister had said after the service. She'd hated their father since the day he'd left.

It all felt like a lifetime ago, thought Soren. But he was back there now. He'd kept the box of figurines for a while, but then, as he and Hana moved from apartment to apartment, the box had gone missing. They'd lost a lot of things in their moves, but never noticed until the missing things were long gone.

EVENTUALLY, HANA CAME BACK from the pool. She found Soren sitting on the couch in the exact same position he'd been in for an hour. "Why are you crying?" she asked. She'd wrapped her long, wet hair in a towel and was now drying it vigorously.

Soren was surprised. "I have no idea," he said. "Really, I didn't know I was."

"Come on," she said. "Let's go to bed."

What he'd been thinking about was how horrible those fish had tasted. He'd received his last one the day before his wedding to Hana. The fish had been delivered to his work by the office courier, wrapped in a business envelope, no big deal apparently. He'd shut the door and killed and eaten it as quickly as he could. No one at work noticed, which was a small miracle. There was nothing in the fish's stomach, though, and despite being shaken by the unexpected appearance of this fish, Soren was almost disappointed that this was the case. There were no more deliveries. The wedding had gone off without a hitch.

What have I missed? he thought. But no answer came to him.

"Did they like the story?" Hana asked.

"I think it might have been confusing," said Soren. They were in bed now, just looking at the ceiling. "One of these days," he said, "that ceiling tile is going to come loose and fall on my face."

Hana laughed. "Then you shouldn't sleep with your mouth so open," she said.

Soren and his wife intertwined as they normally did when the day was over and they were inviting sleep into the house—she turned her back to him and scooted in close, and he draped his arm over hers. She would leave her reading light on until the last possible minute; he would be asleep well before then. He felt her small warm body close to his and saw them, suddenly, as animals in some timeless old forest.

"Hey, did you hear that?" he said.

"Hear what?" said Hana. Her eyes were shut and she was halfway to wherever she was going.

"Never mind," said Soren. But the sound continued— it was a sort of white noise, at first like the drone of a distant engine, then like the shush of whispering, low, not unlike a refrigerator's hum. His sons were tucked in down the hall, safe, safe . . . in the morning perhaps he would touch their sleeping faces, but for now he closed his eyes and tried to concentrate on what he was hearing. Finally, he recognized the sound as it crossed the bedroom; it was the radio from the *Josephine*, tuned to the weather station. *Swell from the south*, it said. There was laughter, and then the slap of fish on the deck. Then he smelled his father's cigarettes and tasted the aluminum tang of beer from a cold can. There, the ocean and their close sleeping

quarters, the old mildewed cushions. He felt the bed roll slightly. And then, finally, clear as a bell, saying *Hold the net, don't lose them, that's it, that's it, that's it*, he could hear his father's voice.

"One more thing," Hana said, sleepily. "Before you got home, the boys were drawing together. One was telling the other what colors to use and what to draw, and then they'd switch." She pulled Soren's arm more tightly over hers. "The pool tonight was empty. There was no one else. It was perfect. And when I was underwater, with my eyes closed, I kept hearing one say to the other: 'Green, now yellow, now blue.'" She coughed. "They were being patient. They were listening to each other. They were drawing us a new apartment. It was the sweetest thing," she said, and then she turned off the light.

THE BABY
\\\\\\\\\\

THE WEATHER OUTSIDE is feral and snow-clotted. And
when the doctor says hold the baby, they do.

They're in the emergency room. The baby has thrown
a fever, he seems to be changing, and that's why they've
brought him in, through the Oregon winter, at this time
of night.

Now everyone is worried.

Did he have these before? These slits? the doctor says.
He points to the side of the baby's neck with the ballpoint
pen that usually lives in his breast pocket.

No, Clare says. Those are new.

Hold him so he sits up, the doctor says. He is on one

side of the hospital bed, and they, Sean and Clare, are on the other.

The baby is between them, crinkling the hospital paper.

THE BABY IS FIVE WEEKS OLD and has almost no hair at all. Earlier he'd been lethargic, ashen. They could barely recognize him. But now he seems fine. A male nurse has given him sugar water from a plastic capsule, and this has perked him up. He is alert and chirping now, moving his arms straight up and down as if practicing a swim-stroke or signaling a truck on the road.

He seems okay, Sean says.

This is just a precaution, the doctor says. Sometimes you get a baby who breathes out of those slits. That's fine. That's within normal. We're worried about the things we can't see.

The room is curtained, and large, impassive machines, pushed against the wall, bulk into the patient area like sleeping watchmen powered down. He, Sean, assumes they are life-giving, used in emergency situations, but their screens are blank, so he doesn't really know.

Ready? the doctor says. He had warned them about the needle, but still it is a surprise to see it. It looks obscene.

They nod and prop the baby up so his back is to the doctor, coo to distract him. They see the pain flash across his face and it registers as their pain before he cries out. But the squall passes quickly, and as soon as the doctor's face relaxes, they take him into their arms and bounce him around.

He is their first, and hadn't come easily.

Is that hard to do? Sean asks the doctor. He means threading a large needle into the back of his child and finding the fluid that will give them the information they require.

Not really, the doctor says. But he is sweating.

When he leaves, a young woman parts the curtains and stands at the foot of the bed. She's holding a clipboard.

Would you say the care you received today has been satisfactory, unsatisfactory, or exceptional? she asks.

Exceptional, Sean says.

Did this baby come from your vagina, the young woman asks, or from a kit?

Who are you? Clare says. She's holding the baby, gently stuffing his arms back into his pajamas.

The woman checks her clipboard and makes a quick apology. Wrong room. She disappears.

THE BABY FALLS ASLEEP on Clare. He's changing, she says.

How? Sean asks.

He's getting heavier, she says.

His little slits are quietly clapping open and shut.

They wait and wait for someone to tell them what will happen next. Eventually the male nurse from earlier comes in.

Angels when they sleep, he says.

Do you have kids? Sean asks.

Oh, no, he says. Not me. He tells them to grab their stuff and follow him to the NICU.

What stuff? Clare says.

The male nurse seems confused. He looks around and

sees no stuff. He checks his clipboard. Yup, his head seems to say.

Well, he says, follow me anyway.

The new room has a television, a small crib, and more sleeping machines. On the walls there are comforting paintings, fat ships in calm seas. In one corner is a large chair. With a flourish, the male nurse shows them how it folds out into a bed.

Voilà, he says, and leaves.

THEY TUCK THEIR BABY, still sleeping, into the crib. They'd followed the male nurse through empty corridor after empty corridor. They'd turned: left, right, left again. An elevator dinged. Left, left, right, and then he'd swiped the door with a card, and they'd followed.

Where is everyone? Clare asks, now that the three of them are alone. There are no clocks or windows in the room and therefore it feels like there is no time in the room. In their hurry, they'd left their phones at home in the kitchen.

We should sleep, Sean says.

Sleep! Clare says. The lighting in the room is industrial and hums a fluorescent tune. Neither of them can find a switch to turn it off, but the baby doesn't seem to mind. He's decided on sleep. He's powered down.

THEY KNOW IT'S MORNING when a doctor opens the door and says Good Morning. This doctor is a young woman. She's holding a clipboard.

The tests are going well, she informs them, but they are inconclusive. They will need to run more tests before discharge.

Why is he still sleeping? Clare says. Why isn't he hungry?

It's natural, the doctor says.

More doctors come into the room, but no one will answer any questions about the baby. Sean and Clare want to know what will happen next, and why their baby is changing so rapidly. The only thing that anyone will say is that they will have to stay in the hospital for a little while longer while more tests are run. The baby sleeps through all of it. The male nurse walks in.

Whoops, he says. Wrong room.

Why won't anyone tell us what's wrong? Clare says.

Well, he says, these doctors? They're also scientists. They believe in certainty. They don't really like to guess at things.

How long have we been here? Clare asks.

The male nurse checks his wristwatch. Two days, he says.

It doesn't feel like it's been two days, Sean says.

I hear that a lot, the male nurse says.

WHEN THEY'RE ALONE, Clare cries. I'm going to wake him up, she says. She means their baby. I'm going to wake him up and we're going to leave.

I don't think that's a good idea, Sean says. We don't know anything.

No one knows anything, Clare says. She's not crying anymore. She picks the baby, who is still sleeping, up from the crib and puts him to her breast. His eyes flutter but he won't open his mouth. Both of them notice that the baby's skin has become slightly scaly. Not like a snake's, but not unlike a snake's.

Come on, Clare says. She rubs his head and his skin goes back to normal.

A small alarm goes off and suddenly there is a nurse with red hair in the room. She looks at Clare disapprovingly.

We get signaled when the babies leave their cribs, she says. There are sensors in the mattress.

When does he eat? Clare says.

This is a hospital, the red-haired nurse says. She takes the baby from Clare and eases him back on the crib's mattress. The alarm stops. We'll take care of that, she says. You should try to relax.

Are you a mother? Clare says. Are you asking me to relax?

The red-haired nurse sighs. You're not here for nothing, she says. If you need to hold a baby, we can get you a baby to hold. But this baby needs to stay on this mattress. She looks at Sean as if to say, this is your responsibility too, to keep the baby in the crib.

Sean nods as if to say, Roger that.

When the nurse leaves, they stand near the crib's rail and watch his little chest move up and down. He's sleeping with his arms over his head like he's being stuck up in the Old West. The slits on his neck are still there, but now they look red and sore.

I don't like any of this, Clare says. Some of this I expected. But not *this*. She gestures toward the baby in the crib, whom they can no longer hold.

Maybe we should turn on the television, Sean says. But when he picks up the remote it doesn't work. He pushes all the buttons he sees but still nothing happens. Finally, he finds a different remote and uses that. Christmas music comes through the ceiling speakers, but the television remains cold and off.

Silver Bells, Sean says after listening for a moment. He recognizes the song because he sang it in school when he was younger. He has a memory of his grandmother in the audience, listening to him sing with her eyes closed and crying.

Please turn that off, Clare says. It's not even Thanksgiving.

THE DOOR OPENS, and in walk four doctors. They are dressed exactly alike, as if they are in a movie called *Doctors*. One of them is the doctor they saw in the emergency room. An older doctor nudges him forward and says, Go on.

I'm sorry, he says. But I need to use the needle again.

Why? Clare says.

I didn't do it right, the doctor says, and we need to be sure.

Well, Clare says, that's not happening. But Sean talks to her in one of the corners of the room, and then holds her as the older doctors instruct the younger doctor, who is gripping a needle that looks different—wider—than the first needle. All four of the doctors are hunched over the baby's crib like crows looking at their own reflections in a puddle.

Oh, the younger doctor says. I get it now.

This is outrageous, Clare says as they finish up.

I understand why you feel that way, the older doctor says. He points at the doctor they'd seen earlier. But he needs to learn.

Let me go, Clare says to Sean. But by the time she is free the doctors are gone. The baby is still asleep, though undressed. His face is signaling calm weather ahead. There are two small pricks of blood on the back of his ribcage like punctuation marks. Clare threads his sleeping arms into his pajamas, checks his diaper, threads his legs, then zips him up and sits down heavily on the chair-bed.

He looks older to me, she says.

Sean doesn't understand what she means until he looks in on the baby. He does look older, though it's impossible to say how.

A young woman parts the curtains and stands at the foot of the bed. She's holding a clipboard.

Would you say the care you received today has been satisfactory, unsatisfactory, or exceptional? she asks.

Exceptional, says Sean.

SOMETIME LATER, their old friend the male nurse saunters in.

Why is our baby sleeping so much? Clare asks him.

All babies sleep, the male nurse says. They have to. It's how they recharge to face a complicated world they know nothing of.

That's condescending, Clare says from the chair-bed. She's lying down with a napkin over her face as if she's trying to keep a headache from spreading.

The male nurse notes something on his clipboard and clicks his pen closed. You'll have to talk to a doctor, then, he says, and leaves.

I'm in pain, Clare says. She's holding her head. I'm having thoughts I'm not proud of.

I'll go get us some food, Sean says.

When Clare says nothing, he takes it to mean that food is a good idea.

THE NURSE AT THE LARGE DESK near the locked door is wearing blue scrubs that have the word Tuesday printed all over them. There are Christmas lights hung haphazardly over the top of her computer. On the screen, little toasters with wings flap around in diagonal patterns.

Is there a cafeteria in this hospital? Sean asks.

And good morning to you, she says without looking up.

Hallways give way to hallways that give way to sucking doors that give way to elevators. Every wall is beige. Every doctor he passes look bored and stands at computer terminals like he or she is gazing into the deep distances of the mind. I'm definitely lost, Sean thinks. When he is about to give up hope he sees a McDonald's.

You look tired, the McDonald's guy says when he places his order.

Thank you, Sean says.

He orders for Clare and then eats two cheeseburgers next to an enormous Christmas tree that sits atop a mountain of perfectly wrapped presents. Outside, the snow is waist-level. It seems to him that he's been here before. Or

that they've been in the hospital for a very long time. Two doctors, one old and one young, sit down next to him.

And *that's* a conversation you never want to have, the older one says to the younger one. Sean strains to listen, but the doctors notice and clam up.

Where have you been? Clare says when he gets back She is frantic, with the light of great knowledge in her eyes.

What'd I miss? Sean says.

She gestures to the baby. He's hooked up to a large machine. A small tube is taped to his arm. One end of the tube is fixed to the machine; the other end goes into his armpit.

It's for food, Clare says. The baby is still sleeping like an angel. But something is different about the way his eyes are closed. Sit down, she says to Sean. He sits and watches as she blinks her eyes, closes and opens them again.

What am I looking for? Sean says.

Just then a box of Kleenex lifts off the counter and floats slowly across the room. Are you doing that? Sean says, but Clare doesn't answer. The Kleenex box comes to a hovering stop just in front of Sean's face. Then it drops from the air into his lap.

I'm changing too, Clare says.

I can see that, Sean says.

One of the paintings comes off the wall and glides gently around the room. Cabinets open and shut. The remote spins like a top on the side table. Does it hurt to do that? Sean asks.

Yes, Clare says. No. It's too complicated to explain. I'm exhausted.

She crosses to where he is and sits down. She lays her head on his shoulder. Her head feels like a huge rock of some kind, as though there's suddenly extra gravity in the room. He flips his arm around and gives her back a small double pat. They'll figure things out, he says.

I don't know about that, she says.

The machine connected to the baby beeps and comes to life. It purrs and hums, and they watch as a heavy beige liquid is pushed through the coiled tube. The baby raises his arms and drops them. He's not smiling, but he's not frowning either. His small face is perfectly relaxed.

I think they're going to put him in water, Clare says.

I had some food for you, Sean says, but I don't know where it is now.

I'm not hungry anymore, Clare says.

THEIR OLD FRIEND the male nurse walks in with a young girl who could be his child. Who moved everything around in here? he asks when he opens the door.

The child is holding a clipboard. Would you say your stay here has been satisfactory, most satisfactory, or exceptional? she asks.

Exceptional, says Sean.

What a winter we're having, the male nurse says. He has a beard now, long and unkempt.

Where'd that beard come from? Sean asks.

I lost a bet, the male nurse says.

I imagine you did, Clare says.

THAT NIGHT, Sean dreams of a huge cathedral bell that has no tongue. He knows in the dream that he's in South America, and that the swinging bell will never sing because he has the tongue in one of the bags he's left at his hotel.

Clare is in the dream too, but she won't turn to face him. They've been walking through mountains for months, and now here they are, at the top of this cathedral.

Some monk in the lower level of the cathedral is tugging on the rope, confused. It's his job to ring this bell, but no matter what he does he only hears the wooden joists creaking with the bell's movement. This sound announces nothing to the city, whose people depend on the bell to tell them when to leave their houses and when to stay.

When he wakes up, a trashcan is hovering over his legs. There is also a new machine near the crib, but this one is connected to the baby's foot.

Sorry, Clare says, and the trashcan bobs gently back to its place under the sink. She's standing in front of one of the paintings, looking through it like a window.

We're not supposed to touch him at all anymore, she says. Just so you know.

IN THE HALLWAY outside their room there is a commotion that sounds like a drawer of forks being dumped onto a marble countertop. Sean leaves the room to investigate. He's come to know this hospital very well. At the far end of the corridor near the nurse's station a large group has gathered. What's happening? he asks when he joins the group.

The man next to him is dressed like Santa Claus. He points to a young doctor who has his hands on his flushed cheeks and is crying. It's the doctor they saw when they first came to the hospital with the baby.

He's getting married, the man says. Finally.

The doctor is hopping up and down with happiness. He is trying to address the gathered crowd, but everyone is cheering and clapping too loudly for Sean to hear what he is saying.

He's not a very good doctor, Sean says.

Everyone is entitled to an opinion, the man says, and continues clapping.

As Sean looks around the group, he sees that everyone's there. The older doctors, the younger doctors. Their friend the male nurse and the child with the clipboard, the guy who works at the McDonald's. Other parents with other babies. Some of these babies are grossly deformed. Some are hooked up to portable machines. Every door on the hall is open.

How did you hear about this? Sean asks the guy standing next to him.

It just sort of occurred, the guy says back.

Then a strange thing happens. As Sean looks around, he discovers that above each person gathered, he can see a floating green bar. He's seen these bars before. In video games, they tell you how much life your character has left. At the beginning, the bar is full and humming. As you progress, and take hits, the bar gradually goes down until your character dies and you have to start over.

Are you seeing these green bars too? he asks.

The guy gives him a look that says please stop.

This is horrible knowledge to have, but he can't make the bars go away. Most of the bars are at least half-full, but there are some that are very low. Their friend the male nurse has about a quarter bar of green energy left. The young girl with the clipboard has a full bar and it pulses over her head with fluorescent benevolence. The joyous doctor who is getting married has only a sliver of blinking red hovering above his flushing face, which means that very soon he will exist only in the memories of others. Everywhere he looks are babies in tiny hospital gowns being held by their tired parents.

Turn off, he says. He hits his cheek with the palm of his hand. Restart. Everyone is looking. Turn off! he yells and hits his ear with his fist.

Sir, their friend the male nurse says as he approaches with caution. He moves like he is testing his weight on young ice.

One more hit does the trick and shorts the circuit. The life bars are gone. Many happy returns, Sean says to the young doctor, who nods graciously.

WHERE HAVE YOU BEEN? Clare says when he returns to the room. I figured out the lights.

He is relieved to see no bars above Clare or above the baby. I don't know, he says. Is he still sleeping?

Yes, Clare says. They took away the machines.

He looks and sees that it's true. It's just the two of them now, and the crib. And, of course, the baby.

Is that our baby? Sean says. He's surprised he doesn't know.

Clare nods.

Is that a good thing or a bad thing, about the machines? Sean asks.

They wouldn't tell me, Clare says. She's crying. I think it's better, she says.

She takes his hand and leads him to the chair-bed. She blinks her eyes and concentrates and the lights in the room dim. A blanket floats from one of the cabinets above the sink and covers the two of them.

Watch this, she says.

The television flips on and on the screen comes the story of their life together.

I've seen this before, Sean says. He's joking, of course. Trying to lighten the mood, pretend they're anywhere else. He's never seen anything like this.

Shhh, Clare says.

On the screen, two actors with a passing resemblance to Sean and Clare meet at a supermarket. They go on a date. They fight and have misunderstandings and make up. They have sex and they laugh. They leave their families to move to a new state where they know no one at all. They take pictures of a growing belly and then they are at a hospital very much like the hospital where they are now.

We were good looking back then, Sean says.

Weren't we? Clare says.

The onscreen Sean is feeding onscreen Clare ice chips in the hospital. She is bouncing on a large exercise ball in a great deal of pain. Then she is on her side and the baby is coming. The camera cuts to the waiting room, where two old people are pacing holes in the carpet.

Here we go, Clare says.

The baby appears like a gasping fish and the two actors open their arms and welcome him to the world. They take turns holding him. A purple cord is cut, a car seat is fitted, and they return home to a freshly painted nursery.

But then there is blood in the shower and residual pain in the room. There are nights so long they feel like months. The baby holds a finger. The baby takes a breast. The baby pees in a perfect arc directly onto his own face. The actors do a marvelous job. There is the first walk into the neighborhood, the calls to the grandparents, the perfect happiness that comes only from feeling the weight of the baby, this changing baby, falling asleep on your chest.

Sean feels Clare stiffen slightly beside him, but they keep watching. On the screen, the days fall from the calendar. The actors bundle for winter, take pictures in the snow. Then: a mild cough. Then: a waxen complexion. Then: a small fever. Then: a worrisome fever. The baby no longer looks anything like himself. The actors bundle the baby and rush him through a winter storm. At the hospital the young doctor is still alive, points to the baby's new slits with his quivering pen, and tries his best with the needle. They follow a male nurse down beige hallways, and the baby is hooked up to machines. No one will give them the answers they want. The actors break character and address the camera. The old film begins to deteriorate, reverse, and play forward. The time stamp evaporates. There are no more exterior shots, no sweeping boom cranes, no tracking shots set to music. The doctors talk to one another in hushed tones and come to decisions. There is nothing but pity and love and suffering and hard facts delivered dispassionately, new machines and old machines, the sound of rubber soles on polished floors and gurney squeaks. They see souls enter the world and souls drift slowly away from the world and souls who cling to the world. There are no windows in the building. The air is thick and clean-smelling. The actors squeeze together on a small chair that folds into a bed and watch on the television the movie of their life, and then the television turns off.

THE ROOM GOES FULLY DARK. Someone is trying the door from the outside, but the door is locked. There's a tentative knock, the sound of a knob being twisted back and forth.

Should we watch it again? Sean says.

No, Clare says. I just want to stay like this. I want him back.

There's a louder knock at the door, and muffled talking. The baby is sound asleep.

They'll say there's been a mistake, Sean says. That's what I've been thinking about.

The dark in the room has taken on weight. The sounds at the door are getting louder.

Clare pulls the blanket to her chin. The baby looks perfectly at peace.

I would empty the world, she finally says. There is nothing I wouldn't do.

IT SEEMS THAT EVERYONE in the hospital is outside the door to their room, trying to get in. The male nurse. The young doctor, and the child with the clipboard. The two older doctors, finally prepared for the conversation they'd been putting off. It sounds, now, like someone is hammering at the door with a mallet. The hinges are starting to pull from the frame.

We don't have much time, Sean says.

I know, Clare says.

Across the room, the crib begins to shimmer and glow. The baby floats up and away from the mattress until he is above the rail. Even if he is never coming back, Sean thinks, he was ours. Clare is not so eager to please. Now the baby hovers in space. He is still sleeping. He begins bobbing slowly toward them to nestle in the crook they've made with their arms.

When he settles down, he is heavier than either could imagine. His breathing is regular. He's having the dream of dreams. He is thinking of fat ships on a placid sea.

Hello? Hello? someone is shouting from the hallway.

Don't wake him, Sean says.

Boo, Clare says. And the baby opens his eyes.

POOLS, I AM A HAWK
\\\\\\\\

IT WAS SUMMER. The trees—brown, bare sticks during winter—were suddenly full and verdant; heat shimmered off the asphalt. School was out, long gone, flushed like a memory of being sick. It would come again, Emily thought sadly, but for now, the timeless, languid world beckoned. Earlier, her little brother Sean had protested sunscreen application and nearly driven their mother to tears as she said, "Please, please, just your cheeks," and Emily thought they'd never leave the apartment. They were in the car now. The pool was open, and their mother had promised they could swim.

At a stoplight, Emily watched as a mother duck wandered across the street with ducklings in tow. "Just like our book!" her own mother exclaimed as her brother sulked in the hot back seat. He sulked, and then he nodded off. Through the window, Emily watched as the mallard paid her ducklings no mind; she waddled to the curb and just kept going. "Hmmm," her mother said, but Emily wasn't listening. She been imagining the pool, but now she thought of Mr. Garrity and what he'd said to her on the last day of music class; one of his awful songs was in her head: "His Eye Is on the Tiny Bird." He'd turned off the classroom lights and she'd run out the door. But now that it was summer and she was getting older, she would let nothing frighten her. On that point she was determined. *Clear*, she thought. The song went away.

The pool they were going to was across town at a club. It was invitation only. "Are we lost again?" Emily asked her mother. It felt like they'd been in the car for hours, and the windows were stuck. Her mother said of course not, but Emily knew they were, because her mother kept pulling over to check her phone. Right, left, left again. The car was an oven. They were in a neighborhood Emily hadn't seen before. The houses were much larger, set off the road, blindingly white in the late morning sun. Tall oak trees lined the block like ancient sentinels.

"Wake up, Sean," her mother called from the front. "Emily, wake him up."

"Why?" Emily said.

"Because if he sleeps now, he won't sleep later."

Sean was three and a half. They shared a room, which Emily thought was ridiculous. For her tenth birthday, she'd asked for her own room, but her parents had bought her a sprinkler attachment. It didn't work and no one even noticed. She shoved Sean hard to wake him up, but he just shifted in his seat, moved further away from her so she couldn't reach him without unbuckling.

Finally, the car stopped for good and Emily's mother got out. Through the car window, Emily could see the tan clubhouse and the gate they were supposed to walk through to get to the pool. There was a tall white fence around everything. She opened her door and stood near her mother while she helped Sean's fat feet into his sandals.

"Ducks eat hay," Sean told Emily.

"That's not right," she said back, and that was the end of the conversation. Her mother handed her a heavy bag full of rolled towels and sunscreen and led the way through the parking lot. Sean reached for Emily's hand because there were cars around, and Emily happily took it. They swung their hands back and forth like they were walking through a meadow, where no parents dared to tread.

At the clubhouse gate, her mother became flustered again. While she made a phone call, Emily and Sean sat on a bench near the entrance. Other kids with towels slung over their shoulders looked at them curiously as they walked by, as though they'd never seen anyone sit on a bench before. Finally, a woman showed up. She was wearing sunglasses and looked glamorous, as if she sat by pools like this every day. "I'm sorry," she said to Emily's mother. "I thought they'd just let you in." Trailing behind her was Nathan, a kid from Sean's class. When Sean saw him, he jumped off the bench and the two boys hugged.

"It's no problem," Emily's mother said.

"That's so cute," the woman said. She was looking at the two boys.

"Isn't it? All I hear all day is *Nathan, Nathan, Nathan*." Now the boys were holding hands and singing a song they both knew.

The woman already knew Emily's name, which made her happy. She smelled like a fashion magazine and when she walked, she placed one foot directly in front of the other.

They followed her through the gate, down some steps, and through a garden. Nearby, people were playing tennis. The air smelled like food frying. The pool was bigger than Emily had expected—a long rectangle, clear water. There were two diving boards, one high and one low: children lined up and ran off the low board without bouncing, some with goggles, all shrieking in pleasure at being so conveyed into water on such a morning. Her mother took Sean into the family changing room, but Emily insisted on changing by herself in the women's room. "Come right out," her mother said, as though she wouldn't have.

The changing room was silent and dark. The wet floor was cold, and the air smelled like chlorine. An older woman sat naked on one of the benches, tending to her feet. "Don't mind me," she said. Emily didn't. She found a locker and carefully unpacked her bag. "Are you one of the Domini kids?" the woman asked when Emily was in her suit.

"No," Emily said. "I'm Emily."

"Oh," the woman said, and went back to her feet.

Once outside, she had no trouble finding her mother.

They were sitting—her mother, the woman, and the two boys—between the large pool and a smaller pool, one Emily hadn't seen, which was clearly for children. Her mother was talking a mile a minute, and the woman was nodding with a straight mouth, now and then saying *good* or *I didn't know that, no.* Her mother didn't say anything to her as she came over and put her towel down. The two boys were sharing French fries. Emily was embarrassed for her mother, but didn't know why she should be.

The line for the small board was long, and other kids kept cutting in, but Emily endured. This wasn't her pool, she knew—she was just a visitor. All the other kids seemed to know one another. She didn't want to attract any attention. When it was her turn, the girl behind her said, "But you haven't even been in the water yet."

"No," Emily said. "I haven't."

"You're supposed to shower," the girl said, but Emily pretended she hadn't heard. She hoisted herself up the steps and cantered until she reached the end of the board. She stopped to see if her mother was watching. She wasn't. "Go!" someone said. Emily plugged her nose and jumped. By the sound of the water, a roar in her ears, she imagined the splash had been big, but no one said anything when she surfaced. She swam calmly and vainly to the ladder, knowing exactly what she might look like to anyone watching.

She'd been worried about the tall board, but it went much the same way. The sign said the board was ten feet, but it felt higher as she climbed the ladder. Water dripped from her suit with every step. At the top, she paused to look around. She was the highest point, she figured, at the club. She could see now that the flowers in the garden were planted in the shape of an anchor. The people lounging on chairs in their bathing suits looked like old floppy seals. She thought about waiting for later to jump, but she didn't know if you were allowed to climb back down the ladder. No one was climbing up behind her, but still. She stayed at the back of the board with her arms on the guardrails until she felt the sun on her shoulders. Her hesitation, she reasoned, was not so much because she was scared of the height, but because she was being thoughtful about how best to land: legs together, arms at her side. She remembered the resolution she made in the car, walked purposefully to the end of the board, and jumped. The water, very flat, very blue, came whooshing up to greet her. The sting on her left arm indicated it hadn't gone exactly how she'd planned, but she was still secretly thrilled at her own audacity.

WITH THAT DONE, she swam in the deep end for a few minutes, hanging on one wall, then hanging on another. In the shallow end, some older kids were dunking one another and splashing. There was a lifeguard, but he was talking to a lady who was leaning up against the base of his chair. The lady's skin was so tan and wrinkled she looked like an ugly crocodile wearing a visor. Somebody was swimming under water, doing laps that way.

Anything goes in *this* pool, Emily thought. She looked for her mother but didn't see her.

With her hands on the side of the pool, Emily took a large breath and forced her head under. The point was to stay submerged as long as she was able. She opened her eyes and began counting in her head. Everything was clear. She could see the bottom of the pool, where the wall gently sloped its corner and became its floor. The almost clear water in the shallow end gradually shifted to blue in the deep end. She walked herself down the wall with her arms. The light flickered near the surface with the swimmers treading water. They were headless now. She looked to where she thought the diving board would be and was pleased when out of nowhere a girl about her age plunged as though from a great height and articulated a *J*; it took her halfway to the bottom of the pool, a pelican movement she'd seen on the Nature Channel, and Emily watched as the girl held herself tight, then opened in the water like a blossom to kick her way to the surface. She made no sound. Directly below her, Emily saw a flash of silver she knew was a small quivering coin; she also knew it was too deep for her to dive, and at this point her lungs were ready to burst anyway. She counted to seven, and when her vision began to pulse dark, she finally let herself up and took a gulping breath. At this, a woman sitting near the pool said *oh my* out of sheer surprise, but otherwise no one else seemed to notice that Emily had been there and then been gone. No one had seen how long she'd been under, but she knew it was a personal record. When she came back to where everyone was sitting, she was surprised to see that her towel was still at her mother's feet. She unrolled and spread it on a white reclining pool chair.

A large hawk was circling above them. Emily squinted into the sun to follow him. "There's a hawk," she said, but her mother wasn't listening. The two boys were raising a ruckus in the toddler pool, whacking at each other with inflatable swords. Some invisible switch had been flipped on the day, and it was now almost unbearably hot. The woman was talking to her mother about private school, and her mother was nodding. Emily closed her eyes and tried to imagine what the hawk saw, but all she could think about was how she looked on her reclining chair. She squeezed her eyes tighter until stars flickered across her lidded darkness, and then she saw it as he would: a flash at the bottom of the pool, her bright coin. He'd never get it.

"He was looking at the young girls," the woman was saying when Emily tuned back in. "He had sunglasses on, so it was hard to tell."

"Who was?" Emily said.

"No one," her mother said.

At her mother's suggestion, then, Emily stood and walked over to where the two boys were playing in the shallow water. On her way, she passed an older boy in a crimson bathing suit. She could tell he was watching her. The concrete had been heated by the sun and burned her feet, but she knew that skipping would look undignified, so she cleared her mind and concentrated only on each foot as it met the walk. She raised her eyes to meet his, but he looked away quickly.

"Hi, Emily," Sean said, when she'd let herself through the gate. The toddler pool was wide and round, but shallow, and Emily stood on the edge of it.

"Do you want to go home?" she said.

"No," Sean said sadly, because he thought Emily was there to gather him up. Nathan came up behind him then and poked him in the ribs with the tip of his inflatable sword. "Aieeee!" Sean screeched, and then the two of them were off, chasing each other in a high-kneed and kicking way around the pool. There were other kids, but they didn't appear as comfortable in the water as these two, and seemed to resent the churn they were turning up.

Imagining herself in a play, Emily thought: now I will enter the water. And she stepped in. The water was warmer here than in the bigger pool. She walked around in a large circle, made the perimeter with her arms out. "I'm a gliding hawk," she said to the boys, but they didn't care at all.

She knew that if she went into the center of the pool and just stood still long enough, they would come to her. So that's exactly what she did. Some parents were slapping sunscreen on one another near the gate. A rhythmic *pock-ing* sound carried over from the tennis courts, leisurely percussive, the clean sound of old age. The water level was at mid-thigh for her, but waist-level for the boys, who had indeed drifted toward her in case she knew something about being in this pool that they did not.

"I found a coin in the big pool," Emily said. She explained, "It's treasure beyond our wildest dreams. It'll send us to private school."

She demonstrated how she'd seen the coin by dunking her head in the water and opening her eyes. "You have to hold your breath," she said.

Sean could do it, but Nathan couldn't. "I'll help," she said. "One, two, three." When she'd learned to swim, Ms. Gravrock had held her head under and told her: *now or never, Emily.* So that's what she did with Nathan. When he dunked, she placed her hand on top of his head and held down while she counted. "No coin," he reported, gasping. So they did it again. This time she counted higher, with her hand firmly at the base of Nathan's skull. His hair floated up and waved in the water like seaweed and tickled the top of her hand.

There was a commotion behind her. "Stop!" someone yelled, and then there was a whistle. Emily knew immediately that both were directed at her. She was mortified. She turned around and saw an angry man, still dressed, splashing toward her in the pool.

"What are you doing?" he said. His face was red and streaked with sunscreen. Emily thought he might hit her; suddenly she couldn't move or talk. He picked Nathan up in his arms. Nathan coughed twice like a seal. "Put me down," Nathan said. "Don't do that," the man said sharply to Emily. He put Nathan down and, unsure what else was required of him, waded away. A woman with a concerned look on her face stood near the side of the pool and held a towel open to welcome him like he was a child. He grabbed the towel and shook it violently. "Nathan, are you okay?" the woman called, but both boys, frightened of the man and unsure who the woman was, had already scampered to the other side of the toddler area, where there was a slide and sandbox.

"He's okay," Emily said. Then, with a slight thrill, she said, "He's my brother."

"He's not," the woman said. She had sunglasses on. "That's dangerous."

No, it's not, Emily thought, but the woman had turned and was following her husband to the great row of shaded chairs that sat under a long blue canopy. Emily sat down in the shallow water, but it seemed like everyone was looking at her, so she stood up and left. *We should go home*, she thought, but then she remembered at home there was nothing to do. They lived in a tiny apartment that cooked in the summer. Their neighbors had recently installed an above-ground pool, but her mom said they didn't want any kids in there for insurance reasons, and Emily wasn't allowed to ask.

The big pool was getting crowded. The line for the low board was long and most of the chairs had been claimed by towels. Emily made a few slow circles around the pool, trying to think of something to do. On the southern edge, there was a low chain-link fence, beyond which was a long manicured lawn that led to the tennis courts. Behind the tennis courts was a row of thick trees. Some older kids chased one another, throwing a tennis ball stuffed into a sock. It arched in the air like a comet. As Emily watched, the group of kids left the sock on the grass and disappeared up a trail into the woods.

It was hard to find her mother because everyone had opened up sun umbrellas. Finally, she heard someone shout "Emily," and she turned to see the woman motioning her over. Her mother barely said anything as Emily lay down on her chair, except to tell her to stay in the shade from now on. The hawk had glided elsewhere, and now nothing interrupted the deep blue-purple of the noon sky, not even the wisp of a cloud, not even a plane. The coin was still on the bottom of the pool, though. No one else had seen it. She had checked.

"WHAT HAPPENED WITH NATHAN?" her mother asked. The other woman was off playing with the two boys. "Someone saw you pushing his head underwater."

Emily pretended she had no idea what her mother was talking about.

"Best behavior," her mother said. "He could've been hurt."

"I was standing right there," Emily said.

"Emily," her mother said, and that was the end of it.

WHEN IT WAS TIME FOR LUNCH, they found the boys and went into a cooled cabana. Everyone was feeling a little sun-sick. After they finished, Emily stayed inside as everyone else went back to the pool. Her mother had quietly told her not to mope; but she wasn't moping, she just didn't want to be around the boys or her mother. She'd brought a library book. The woman told her she could order ice cream from the counter and Emily said she might want to do that. When her mother tried to give Emily money, the woman said please not to worry. "Here's the number," she said. "43571—and just tell them you're my guest." Sitting alone at the table now, Emily rolled the number around in her head as though it were some sort of magic marble. *4-3-5-7-1*, she thought. *4-3-5-7-1, and the world opens.* But then she realized she didn't know the woman's name. *Margaret?* she thought. *Esme?* She was so caught up in trying to imagine this woman's name, and what her house might look like, its many rooms and her husband, that she didn't notice the two girls at a table next to hers until one of them sat down across from her. Emily recognized them as part of the group that had been playing with the sock ball on the grass earlier.

"What's your name?" the girl asked. She was wearing a bikini and her long hair was darkly flat and stringy, like it had recently dried in the sun. The other girl stared at the two of them.

Emily didn't answer. Then she said, "I'm here with my mom."

"Do you belong here?"

"Yes," Emily said. "43571."

"We're not going to tell on you," the girl said. "You look like someone, that's all." She adjusted the shoulder strap of her red bathing suit and looked at her friend.

"Everyone looks like someone," Emily said.

"Yes," the girl said. "But not like this. Not in *this* way."

Emily didn't say anything.

"You look like *her*," the girl whispered.

"Like who?" Emily said.

"We're not supposed to say her name," the girl said.

Emily looked at the other girl. She was maybe one or two years older. She wasn't smiling. She'd been joined at her table by two boys, neither of whom wore shirts. "We've been watching you all day," the girl across from her said. "Come sit with us," she said. "You can sit at our table."

"Don't sit," the other girl said. "Let's just show her."

The girl at Emily's table looked at her friend. Something passed between them that Emily couldn't read. The two boys had already stood. They were in their bathing suits too. One of them had defined muscles, but the other one was fat, his belly button like a dark cave. "Show me what?" Emily said.

RATHER THAN WALKING THROUGH the pool area, they walked out a side door in the cabana. The path led them through the garden, and past an outdoor patio Emily hadn't seen before. They passed a shuffleboard court. When they reached the lawn, Emily looked back for her mother but couldn't see her beside the pool. The place was very crowded now, and loud children jumped into the water at both ends, throwing tennis balls at one another. She did see Sean and Nathan—they were on the swings near the toddler area—but if they saw her, they made no indication.

The girl who had summoned Emily was walking quickly now, followed by the other three. They were slouching their shoulders as if they didn't want anyone on the tennis courts to see them. No one had said anything to Emily since they'd left the cabana, though they kept looking behind them to see if she was still there. A little beyond the tennis courts, Emily could see a chain-link fence with a small, unwoven section near one of the posts.

Beyond the fence was the woods. They held open the fence for Emily, and she followed. Once she was on the other side, the world was a little quieter, and the air colder. The woods seemed to muffle the sound of the day.

"How much further?" Emily asked.

"Farther," the girl in front corrected her.

"Farther?" Emily said.

"Not much," she replied.

It felt strange to Emily to be in her bathing suit in the woods, but everyone else was too. The dirt path poked and scraped at her bare feet, but she was determined to keep up. She felt very far away from her mother and brother. She liked that they had no idea where she was. She would never tell them. The path snaked and turned and then disappeared below her feet, but the others kept on in front of her. Sometimes one of them reached out to touch a tree lovingly as they passed.

The woods were getting thicker. The sun barely peeked through. Eventually the group stopped and formed a semicircle. When Emily caught up, she saw what they were looking at: a small shrine at the base of a large tree.

The shrine was a small, wooden box, decorated with glitter and feathers and tiny writing that Emily couldn't read. The girl turned and stared at her. "You look just like her," she said. She crouched down near the tree. Emily could see the girl's spine protruding from her skinny back. She could've counted her ribs if she'd wanted to. The girl opened the box and pulled out a school photograph. She stood and looked at one of the boys, and then held the photograph in front of her like she was about to give a presentation.

It did look like Emily. "Who is she?" Emily said.

"Dead," the fat kid said.

"We come out here and think about her," the girl said. "And try to talk to her. We thought maybe you could help, because you look so much like her."

"What is it you want to know?" Emily said.

"Who did it," the thin boy said. "We want to know who did it."

"Her name was Claire Domini."

"How did she die?" Emily asked. They told her. "Oh," Emily said.

"It's the worst thing you could imagine," one of the girls said. Her mouth was a thin, drawn line. For a while no one said anything. Emily didn't like the way they were looking at her. She adjusted her swimsuit.

"If you are Claire's ghost, you have to tell us," said the fat boy

"I'm not a ghost," Emily said.

"Here's what we'll do," the girl said. And she proceeded to take everything out of the box and arrange it on the ground: Claire's school picture, a piece of cloth that looked to Emily like it came from soccer shorts, another picture, a small figurine. There was clearly an order to this. The girls took their time in arranging the objects while the boys watched. A breeze washed through the woods and disturbed the piece of cloth—one of the boys chased it down. Then everyone stood in a circle and began to hum. "Come on," the older girl said, and made room for her. Emily didn't want to move, but they had chosen to include her, and she stepped forward. She tried to follow the tune, but could not, so she hummed softly with her eyes closed. She focused on the vibration in her teeth. Soon she imagined she was on the edge of a large sandy cliff and opened her eyes. Everyone was looking at her. The girls held hands and then dropped them. Then they pressed the palms of their hands to one another's chests. No one reached for Emily, but that was okay with her.

One of the boys held up a dry leaf, and solemnly lit it on fire with a small lighter he'd dug from his swim trunks. The girl who had first approached Emily looked euphoric and sad. The older girl began to sob like she was in a play. Soon everyone was crying, and Emily tried to make herself cry too, but she couldn't.

"You look like her," one of the girls told Emily. "You should probably cry if you can."

Emily shook her head. But then, to her great relief, the tears did come. "I'm sorry about your friend," she said to the chubby boy, who seemed the saddest of the group.

"Thank you," he said.

"Ugh," the older girl said. "It didn't work."

"I told you," the other girl said. "I said."

The older girl looked at Emily and then at the chubby

boy. "She wants to touch you, you know," she said and laughed. "She wants to put her finger right in your belly button."

"No, she doesn't," he said. Then he reached for Emily and hugged her.

"You're hugging a ghost," the girl said. She was laughing now. "She's an impostor. She's going to haunt you."

"I don't care," he said. "I don't care at all."

Eventually the ceremony was over, and the girls carefully packed everything into the box. They walked back through the woods in silence. Emily thought she wouldn't have known the way back, but she was sure of herself now, and the path to the tennis courts was clear; the pocking of the racquets came louder until finally they were at the fence, then through it. The chubby boy had searched once for her hand as they walked, and Emily had let him take it. His palms were sweaty. There was a warmth and softness to his touch.

When they passed the pro shop, one of the girls picked up a tennis ball sock from the grass, and their game began. Emily didn't know the rules. You swung the sock in rapid circles and launched it up as high as you could, apparently. Then someone else retrieved it and did the same. "You're out," one of the girls screamed. She was looking at Emily. "You're out," she said again. "You have to go to the pool." Emily looked toward the pool, bristling now with life, and then looked toward the girl. She wanted to stay with them. "You're *out*," the girl said. "I won't tell," Emily said. The girl laughed. One of the straps to her bikini had slipped, and she thumbed it back into place. "You can't keep a secret," she said. "I can see it in your face." *Yes, I can*, Emily thought, and began to protest but the girl had already turned her attention back to her friends. Emily could feel the sun on her shoulders again, warming her. The boy who had reached for her hand now took the sock and launched it as high into the air as he could. Emily watched its parabolic arc, traced it across the blue sky. "That's the rattiest bathing suit I've ever seen," one of the girls said. "Disgusting," said the other one. Emily knew when it was time to go, so she left.

"WHERE'VE YOU BEEN?" her mother said. She was beside herself. "I had everybody looking." Emily could tell she was embarrassed.

"I'm sorry," Emily said.

"You could've been hurt, for all I knew," her mother said. "People drown, even when there are lifeguards."

"Sorry," Emily said again, and that seemed to calm her mother down. She knew no one had actually been looking for her.

"There she is!" the woman said as she approached, with Nathan and Sean in tow. "I told you she was fine."

"I was by the tennis courts," Emily said.

"The tennis courts!" the woman said, as though it was the funniest thing she'd ever heard.

Sean and Nathan were eating popsicles, happy as could be. "Oh," her mother said as Sean came closer. "I should've put on a little more sunscreen." He was as red as a lobster.

"He'll be fine," the woman said, putting her arm around Nathan. "It's time we're off, though. Jim will be back."

Emily's mother was rooting around in her bag for something. She didn't find it. "Thanks for having us," she said. "We had a great time."

"I have to sign you out," the woman said, apologetically.

"Oh! Silly me," her mother said.

At the gate, Sean and Nathan hugged as if they'd never see each other again. "So cute," the woman said, and smiled.

"So, so cute," Emily's mother said.

The car was as hot as a frying pan. They had to put their towels down on the seats. As they pulled out of the parking lot, Emily looked out the streaked car window at the club's gate. She hadn't expected anyone to see her off but was still disappointed to see that no one was there.

AT HOME, THEY HAD DINNER and went to bed. Sean tossed and turned, but finally gave in and went silent. Emily stood eventually and crossed to his side of the small room. His bed was a menagerie of cheap stuffed animals: gaping lions, her old bear. As she untangled him from his blanket so he wouldn't wake later, he cried out "Nathan" one time loudly, and then fell deeply to sleep. His hair was matted, sweaty. The room was hot but not as hot as it had been earlier. They were on the first floor, which helped.

From her own bed, Emily heard her father come home and rummage around in the fridge. The kitchen was next to their room. You could hear everything. Her mother laughed about something. "Rich people," her father said.

"They were nice," her mother said.

Emily waited until they went to sleep. She was used to the night sounds in the apartment: two flushes from the toilet, the hurried rasp of teeth being quickly brushed, the door creak, the click of the bed lamp going off. Everything was so close. Eventually she heard her father's heavy rhythmic snores. The traffic outside her open window died down; the crickets chirped up. She waited twenty minutes more, then stood. Her brother slept on his back, helpless as a lizard.

She walked quietly out of her room, through the kitchen, out the back door. It was surprisingly cool outside. The air smelled like someone was doing laundry next door.

In the backyard of the apartment complex, she stopped to let her eyes adjust. Grass, pavement, telephone poles against a cloudless night sky: shades of darkness, and she, invisible. *I'm a ghost*, she thought. She wasn't worried about being seen. She still had her bathing suit on. No one had checked.

Headlights washed over the grass, swept the side of the building next to hers, disappeared. She moved deliberately through her yard, then across the apartment's small parking lot.

The pool next door had no lights. It was just a big ring of plastic, filled with water. She walked gingerly up the steps and tested the water with her hand. It was still warm from the day. As quietly as she could, she lowered herself in.

The world felt enormous when everyone else was asleep. And this was nothing like the pool at the club: she was swimming in water that was itself above the ground. Standing, the water came up to her chin. She tiptoed to the center of the pool. Once there she took a tremendous breath and fluttered her hands so that she gracefully sat on the bottom, cross-legged. She knew if she opened her eyes, she would see nothing but darkness, so she shut them tighter and soon there it was in front of her: her coin. She counted and counted. When she was done with that, she tried floating on her back, the way she'd learned with Ms. Gravrock. Arms out wide, arched back, ears below the waterline. The trick was to not be afraid, the trick was to believe you could do it, and then you would float. She got it on the second try.

Above her, the stars pricked through the coarse blanket of night. A light in the apartment flickered on, and she was aware of a shadow in its window, watching her. She tried to imagine what she looked like, what she might look like from high above. She was a hawk, gliding, swooping, watching herself. What bad thing could happen to her? Who would protect her? No one even knew where she was. She thought of Mr. Garrity's dry hand on the skin at the small of her back, then up to her shoulders, and the boy who'd hugged her. She remembered all the stupid things her mother had said that day, her dumb nervous laugh. Then she imagined a cold hand reaching for her ankle, pulling her under, tugging her to a scanty shrine in the middle of a dark cave. *Clear*, Emily thought. *Clear*. She was talking to her brain. Water floated deliciously in and out of her ears. *Now, ascend*, she thought. She arched her back until it hurt. One final image came to her, and it was of herself, standing behind Nathan, holding him underwater. She felt his head now, small in her talons, too easy, but she would never. She would never! *Clear!* It worked for a minute.

HOLIDAY
\\\\\\\\

WE HAD COME TO AN AGREEMENT, my wife and I, and so to celebrate we made plans to visit for one week a charming village on the south shore of an English sea. This was her place; she'd found it. She'd circled some photos in a magazine and made all the arrangements. Did we have the money for this? Not close. But it was winter in the Midwest, the bleak season, and we'd spent the better part of the year looking for the river source of our discontent. We thought maybe it was the cold; maybe the early dark; maybe the mountains of never-to-melt snow. Or the culture of reflexive but empty niceness that sifted over the frozen streets of our city like ruthless, cheerful fog. We stretched plastic over the windows in our apartment, smoothed the creases with a hairdryer per the instructions, and plugged every crevice near the doorframe where wood pulled from wall. Still, the cold drafted, it found its way in. Perhaps there are ways to get through winters like this, but whatever they are, we hadn't discovered them, and on the days we did leave the apartment, it felt like we were the only unhappy people in our city.

Here's a joke, our neighbor had said to us one day in the middle of a blizzard (we were all outside, chipping ice from the sidewalk, he must've been trying to buoy us): a Norwegian, he said, will give you directions anywhere in his village, except to his house. We waited, shovels held waist-high, for a punch line that did not come. That's more of a saying, my wife said. He shrugged. It's not to everyone's taste, he said, and went back inside.

You can't blame me for this, my wife said. We'd moved here for her job.

I told her I wouldn't dream of it. But because this was not the life I'd imagined either, of course I did.

Here was our winter: our apartment had been broken into, jewelry taken, so we changed the locks. We bought special UV lamps to mitigate the low light and rearranged the furniture to trick ourselves into thinking we'd moved. Small electric heaters blazed at all times, but still we'd taken to wearing hats in the house and stopped combing our hair. We didn't eat much, because we didn't feel like eating. We'd been married seven years. The hovering spirits were not benevolent ones. Our mornings in that apartment bloomed a strange, acidic silence that held tightly at our throats, and some days we didn't talk at all. We knew the winter was breaking us, keeping us in separate rooms. We were not who we wanted to be.

Was that the only thing pushing against us back then? It couldn't have been, but my memory these days is not what I'd hoped it'd be. I do remember that we were confused as to where money was supposed to be coming from, dispirited by credit card debt that hung like a garlic wreath from our necks. I remember that loneliness was our night-creeper—that we were becoming wary of our own intentions and ability to *follow through*. I was at work on a book that I knew, via the secret door that led to the brain of my heart, would never come out. When I looked at the pages I'd written, it was like cowering before an object of pure entropy, the best lines echoes of better lines from other books. This knowledge was like a bad birdsong in my skull, unrelenting, listless—but I wasn't ready to talk to my wife about it. I'd tried one morning and clammed up. What was I going to say, that I just couldn't get it done? That I couldn't imagine anything beyond what I hadn't managed to make? I'd already lost two books; they'd slipped like sand through my fingers. I think she understood my quiet. She didn't feel like herself either.

Meanwhile, all our old friends were having children. The announcements arrived daily, missives of joy. Most weekends the two of us spent at least part of one day driving around our snow-clogged city, sledding through intersections, chipping ice from the inside of the windshield, looking for clothes for these children we had not met and most likely would not meet, for more often than not these friends had made their homes in cities far away.

One Saturday morning, while grocery shopping, I came

trudging around the aisle with some buy-one-get-one news and caught her cradling a sack of flour like a newborn. I watched. She was looking at yogurts, and swaying slightly, moving on the balls of her feet and rocking gently as she checked prices and made the mental calculations we had become accustomed to making.

My wife is a beautiful woman. These calculations broke my heart. We had played by the rules, and the rules had brought us here, where private despondency was the coin of the realm. What did we want? To dislodge. To redirect. To reclaim something we'd lost. We wanted something no one could take from us, something to fend off the darkness we knew to be approaching. At least: that's what we thought. I said: I caught you cradling that sack of flour. She wasn't shocked. She said: yes, you did.

At Christmas, my wife's parents, who lived far away, and who, if they thought of me at all, thought unkindly, gave her money. We spent it immediately. We bought two plane tickets and a week at a B&B, with a small amount left over. We packed lightly. It was irresponsible. It was a jailbreak. There was music in the air.

And our agreement was this: we'd have a baby, make a home, and be unhappy no more.

OUR FLIGHT TOOK US from the snow hills of Minnesota, cruised low over the continental power grid, and touched down in New York, the city where, years ago, we'd met. We waved through the small window at our younger, more certain selves. The flight to Heathrow was horrendous and bumpy, but still my wife managed to sleep. She rested her head on my shoulder. I tried not to think about my book. The ocean below us seemed a solid thing, an expanse you could draw on.

I took a pill, slept eventually. When I woke, the cabin was dark, and I had the disorienting sensation I was hurtling through someone else's dream. My wife, awake now, watched a nature special with headphones on. The man next to me was snoring, and his labored breath smelled like ginkgo leaves. Out his window there was only a flat darkness and the sound of movement.

The airline—I am not worried about telling you which one it was; it was United—lost all the bags we'd checked. Before we'd left, our cheerful neighbor had stopped by to wish us well, and had announced that if it were *he* traveling internationally, he would learn from his last trip, which was to Granada, Spain, to visit the Alhambra—not a single one of his bags had made it home. So, on account of all the thieves in the world, he'd said dramatically, he would under no circumstances check a bag. Midwesterners love nothing more than to give advice. As I stood at the United counter, trying to pry information from the clerk about when we could expect our luggage, I decided I would write him a postcard. And that postcard would say: you were right! The exclamation point would appeal to him.

There are thieves everywhere. They gave us forty-five pounds to buy clothes and no information about when we could expect our bags. I said: you have wrecked our holiday, and you will be hearing from me. The clerk shrugged.

He knew there was nothing I could do. Ruined, I thought, though we'd packed nothing anyone would want. On our way to the coast in our rented and empty car, my wife kept repeating what I'd said and cracking up. You will be hearing from me, she said in a basso profundo voice. Maybe you don't know who I am now, but you will, and you will be hearing from me.

THE PLACE WE WERE STAYING was called the Captain's House. It was off a skinny little winding street, only two or three blocks from the center of town, which was itself only two or three blocks away from the shore. This was a beach town, but it was January, and everything was for the most part boarded up. We missed the correct turn two or three times, went round the empty town square, and finally found a parking spot directly in front of an ancient-looking Anglican church. There was no sign outside the church that told us we couldn't park there, and no one to ask. I had sweat right through my shirt while driving. I had filled the car with a panicked smell. We said, fine, this is it. It was already very late at night.

I'm not going to describe this house for you yet, because what happened later on is so strange. I'd like you to picture, instead, simply whatever your version of a small English house might look like, a tourist trap B&B near a beach, in a town that depends on the sea for oysters and visitors like us, washed ashore, unclean and unkempt, uncertain, to some degree, about what the future might hold, yet moving toward it, in the hope that the second part of their lives together would soon be granted recognizable shape. That's probably good enough. The man who owned the house, who my wife had corresponded with over the internet, was called M. He answered the door, looked up and down the street, and said: What, no bags? You are the most optimistic Americans I have ever met.

FROM OUR ROOM ON THE SECOND FLOOR, my wife used an international card to call her parents to thank them. I had the sense they weren't happy we'd used the money to book a week at the Captain's House, but what did we care? They were miles away, minor characters. We figured they would be pleased when presented with a grandchild.

That night, after M.—who looked, as my wife pointed out, like an ancient, pecking bird—explained the long history of the house, we stayed up until dawn. We were relieved, I think, and a little delirious from travel, thrilled with the idea of spending money we couldn't afford. The low-ceilinged room was small and drafty but bore no resemblance to our apartment in the Midwest, and what I remember now about that first night was that it felt as though entire swaths of our past life disappeared as if they'd never existed at all. Where was our luggage? We had parted with it; it was not here. And as the night wore on, we became enchanted with the idea that all you had to do, change yourself was to change your context. No letters would find us. It all seemed so easy. My wife stripped off her clothes, and I mine. The bed was narrow, the quilt knitted and thick, a sleep shroud we kicked down to our ankles then recovered as the night settled lightly around us.

From the small window in our room, we could see the

ocean. Near the shore, a solitary nightwalker scuffed his boots in the sand, and, farther out, we saw the lights of a barge bearing out to sea. The hours passed. We sank into them. We talked like we hadn't spoken in months—as though our life up to this point had been a series of private chapters we'd been unable to assemble. With some sadness, I told her about my book drifting away. She listened, and then said she wanted to tell me something she'd never told anyone before.

WHEN SHE WAS YOUNG, she began, she cycled through a series of largely irrational but deep fears in a way that had baffled her parents. One day she was deathly afraid of the peach-colored curtains in the dining room and would not leave the couch until her father took them down. Another day, perhaps, she couldn't hear the sound of her sister practicing scales on the piano without imagining that someone was watching her through the kitchen's screen door. When she was a little older, she had trouble with what she, and the therapist her parents made her see, called "leaving dreams." She would wake up, only to find that a thin strand of her dream life had emerged from sleep with her: a lingering image, an emotional state rendered in sensory detail. An animal she'd dreamed of wanting would lurk in the shadow near her closet, then, as she squinted in the darkness, scurry under her bed. Certain objects became radiant and pulsed: called to her. Then she would wake once again, this time with her mother at her bedside, pressing a hand to her forehead, reassuring her that all was well—See? her mother would say. I've turned on the light, there is nothing wrong. They gave her a set of small, woven worry dolls to put under her pillow. But there are layers between dream life and waking life, she said, and these dolls, which were supposed to absorb her anxiety and bear it away, never did. What did you do? I asked her. I stopped talking for almost a year, she said. I was never entirely certain I was the best judge of what was happening—I became used to things feeling both familiar and strange simultaneously—and I just decided to stop bringing other people into it. When I asked her what had finally shifted, she was quiet for a moment, and I saw her withdraw into herself almost completely. Near the end of the year when she had stopped talking, she finally began, she'd become fixated on a single repeating episode, something in her imagination that reached out to her and crossed into the realm of nightmare, and that was this: that every night, as she got into bed, she became convinced that as soon as she was asleep, someone dressed entirely in black would climb the gutter to her bedroom window, slide it open, creep silently across her bedroom carpet, and stand at the foot of her bed without saying a word. This man, she said, did not mean well, and his power was great. With one breath, he could inhale all the good she'd known and replace it with emptiness. He knew something essential about her that she didn't understand herself; he knew where to find it, and he'd come to spirit it away. Never mind that her house didn't have climbable gutters (she'd checked); never mind that her window was locked. In the middle of the night things are different, and in the middle of the night, the house had gutters, and the man was standing over her, had come to take part of her away, and he was giving her a choice: gaze upon me and know that I'm real, or keep your eyes shut and be left alone. For this reason, she always slept facing the wall, so that when the man came in, and stood near the foot of her bed, he would never know for sure if her eyes were open or shut. If she was asleep, or merely pretending. At some point, out of nervous exhaustion, she really would fall asleep, and wake with the morning. She never told her parents about the visiting man, and one night, almost a year later, she'd chanced it, and opened her eyes. He wasn't there. She'd vanquished him.

I DON'T KNOW WHY I've never told you this, she said finally. Or why I've told you just now.

She reached over and held my hand. It felt, to me, like she was very far away. I'm glad you did, I said.

Don't be surprised, she said. I've never told anyone. No one noticed I hadn't spoken. At least, that's how I remember it. Don't be upset. No one knew. But now you do.

I'm not, I said. I'm not upset.

When I asked her where she thought he'd come from, she shook her head. I don't think, she said, I could describe it for you if I tried. She went quiet. Away, she finally said. It doesn't have an ending.

I cherish stories like this. I go looking for them, and lying there, I felt as if a door had opened and I'd slipped into a new room on the heels of someone else. I wished to know more, but I could tell she'd had enough, was exhausted and done with talking. Every story has a limit, a line that cannot be crossed, and that's where we were—and anyway, I figured, we had nothing but time now that we were here. I could ask her tomorrow, or the next day, as questions occurred to me. She squeezed my hand and brought it to her breast; she wished to come back; I didn't push. I could hear cars on the street now, dull engines revving to life—morning was at the door. We'd come here to think about the people we wanted to be, to look forward, and so that's the direction we faced. Would our son be more like me or her? Would our daughter grow up to be a good person? We stopped thinking about money. It wasn't something that occurred to us then, on that first night. How much of it we would need.

I hope he has your face, she said.

I didn't want that, not for anyone, but I didn't tell her that right then. You'll be hearing from me, I told her later. I was in the bathroom, trying to figure out the flush mechanism. She was sprawled out on our bed.

Say it again, she said. So I did.

THAT FIRST MORNING WE SLEPT LATE, and when we did wake, we watched the sun cut through our small window and move down the wall. Our clothes—we'd washed and wrung them in the sink, set them to dry—hung from their hangers over the bathroom door like empty sacks.

I realized that at some point in the night I'd come to an understanding about my book. The lines had been there, but I couldn't arrange them. I had approached my work

with a shameful passivity and waited so long for meaning to accrue that it simply snatched itself away. I'd been
selfish but not selfish enough; as such, I'd deserved the
crumbling I'd witnessed, for I'd offered no protection and
stood by, watching, as the book drifted from my reach. I
thought of the radiance my wife had talked about in her
dreams. My pages had none of that, and I knew, as surely
as if I'd been told by God himself, that no one would read
them. I felt obliterated, and, for a second, free of this earth.
I thought perhaps I would never again leave this bed nor
this room. But soon my heaviness returned; we grew hungry for lunch and I put these thoughts away.

It turned out that M. had come to own the Captain's
House via what he called a great misfortune. We didn't
press. He'd laid on the dining room table three settings,
and we joined him for soup and homemade bread. This,
he informed us, would be our only meal together, but it
was a courtesy he enjoyed. He was tall, and stooped, and
as he passed the bread around the table he looked only
at my wife. We talked in a small way about nothing for a
while, but I could sense my wife becoming uncomfortable.
I know you, he finally said to her. I think we've met.

This, she said, is our first time in England.

No, he said. Can't be. I remember.

My wife looked at me, and then back at M. She flushed.
By the water, he said. Near the bookstall. When we met,
M. continued, you were carrying a baby.

My wife shook her head.

I'd swear by it, M. said. You let me hold her.

She was tiny, he continued, and dressed for the cold.

You were watching the evening boats come and go. You were waiting for someone. I held her out of the wind. She fit inside my jacket. And you, he said, were so sad.

No, my wife said, and though she managed a smile, I could see she was shocked. No, she said again. She looked pained in a way I'd never seen before. I wanted to step in, to redirect, but I was surprised too and could think of nothing to say. My hands stayed on the table. Presently, M. composed himself, and looked at me with red-rimmed and watering eyes. I was struck still. I had a sense that the house itself was listening closely, hearing something I couldn't—a hidden melody, a warning. Then suddenly he reached across the table and put his hand on top of mine. At this touch I felt a cold pulse run up my arm like an electrical transfer, and I pulled my hand away, perhaps too violently. He gave a small cry; then, composing himself, he picked up his fork to illustrate what was happening to his memory, and apologized profusely. He had, he told us, been thinking of someone else. Of course he had been. You must be the husband, he said. I mumbled yes, and after that, his mood went dark, and he became less talkative.

I don't remember much about the rest of the meal, except that whenever I looked across the table at my wife, she looked at her lap.

Finally, after we had politely eaten our fill and it became clear that our now silent lunch could go on no longer, he raised his glass. To happiness, he said. To health. May it flow, he said, now looking directly at my wife, from this house to your heart.

Thank you, she said. Thank you very much.

And he smiled in a way I will never forget, as though he knew something we did not. I saw sharp, yellowed incisors, the flick of a dry tongue. Then his lips closed, and the feeling was gone.

AFTER WE LEFT THE HOUSE, we wandered the village, and made our way to the shore. And as we walked along the beach, a low fear began to blossom and hum in my chest. After a while, my wife asked if I needed to sit down. I did. She pressed the back of her hand to my forehead. I asked her if she'd been upset at lunch. She told me she'd been startled, but she was fine now, it had been a mistake, he was old. I knew she wasn't telling the truth. We've come all this way, she said. We've come *all* this way. I asked her if she wanted to leave, but she pretended not to hear. She took her hand away from my head. You have a slight fever, she said. She took my hand, placed it in her lap, and began to cry softly. An old lady passed us, and said there, there. Don't look at us, please, I said.

It was just weird, she said. That's all. We watched the waves roll in and out and eventually the oppressive feeling passed. We stood, and did our best impression of a couple, tourists on holiday. We bought postcards. We wrote in our journals. But something was off, tilted. The clouds hung very low and made a flat white ceiling of the sky. Our old unhappiness stranded back to us, braided with something less solid but just as real, and the knowledge that this was happening took physical root, and became a headache that painted the back of my eyes. I had never hallucinated before, but I was feverish, and I saw M. everywhere. He had firmly lodged in my mind. There was a new unbalance to things I didn't know how to address. And it seemed to me like something had been taken from us, but I didn't, for the life of me, know what it was, or how to get it back.

I don't know what my wife was thinking. We didn't eat dinner, and we talked no more. Every turn we took felt like a mistake. We headed back to the Captain's House as the sun was going down. A woman met us at the door and introduced herself as M.'s wife. She told us that M. had told her what he'd said, and wished to apologize, again. He's not well, she said. Her hair was white and cut short. Her face bore the deep lines of suffering.

Please, my wife said. Think nothing of it.

His mind, the woman said as she let us in. He always thinks something terrible is going to happen. He's had, she said as she shut the door behind us, a very hard life.

Please, my wife said again. We're having a lovely time.

That night, my fever climbed and then broke. I dreamed that someone had found our bags, but no one had bothered to tell me. I dreamed of my wife near the water, holding our baby. And then M. was there, picking her up, folding her in his jacket, accusing me of things I had yet to do. Look more closely, he said to me. When I woke, my wife, in all of her beauty, took my hand in hers. She asked how I was feeling, I told her: fine. I was just happy to be feeling better. We made love and I felt a gratitude so great and directionless that it shaded into guilt. This is our holiday, my wife said. It's ours. We don't live here. We're just visiting.

THE NEXT DAY we woke around lunch. M. was nowhere to be found, but we had a key as well as directions, and a small meal had been placed directly outside our door that had most likely been sitting there for hours. Tucked into our door was a map, and a note written in shaky text that indicated there were two bicycles around the corner of the house, which we could use if we so desired. We biked around the town, which was modestly shuttered for the winter, stopping now and then to gape at the butcher shop windows, or go into a bookstore. We found a pub and stepped in. We had decided separately, I think, to reset ourselves, to start again but when I returned from the bar carrying our drinks, my wife said: I don't want you to look at the newspaper.

I could tell by the way she said it she was serious. The paper was on our table. It had been there when we walked in. The article was brief, an obituary for a writer whose work I had, long before I'd met my wife, idolized. I had, I thought, been writing my book for him: mirroring his sentences, his words. But I wasn't, really. I was just lifting. He'd died on Long Island, in the company of his children. It was liver failure. His final gesture, the paper reported his daughter saying, was a gentle fluttering of his hands. I could see it, of course, as incongruous as the image struck me at the time. A bed, tightly made, this man staring out his window at the small boats tugging gently at their anchors in the harbor, the ceaseless folding of the waves. *All life*, he had written in one of my favorite poems, *exists at the expense of other life*. And here he'd gone, shuffling off. My wife said she was sorry. She'd never liked his work, but was polite about it. I said, what can you do? I tried to absorb the information as deeply as I could.

But what *can* you do? Time catches everyone. There's nothing interesting about that, but it cannot be the full story.

We drank our beers in silence, and then biked to the shore. It was afternoon, the low light pushed us forward. We biked together, slowly, without speaking, down the middle of the street. No cars came. It felt to me like we had the entire town, and all of its grayness, all of its January damp and splendor, to ourselves. Perhaps we biked for hours. I felt both diminished and enlarged at the same time. The wind pressed against my face in a pleasing way and cut through my sweater. I pushed some spit from between my lips and let it dry coolly on my chin. I was aware that we, my wife and I, were biking in tandem, and that she might have been lost to herself as well, but our reveries did not overlap. I thought about my parents, and then I thought about their parents. I allowed myself to be borne backward.

We reached a dead end, where pavement gave way to path, some patch of sand that led to the beach. I could smell the ocean. I could hear its echo. We walked our bikes over the shore, and after a few minutes, my wife found a point down the beach she said she'd like to see. She was looking at the wreck of an old oyster trawler. I'll race you, she said. She dropped her bike in the sand and began running. Though I knew better, I swung my leg over the seat, placed my feet in the pedals, and began to churn after her. The wheels turned, but the bike would not go forward, not an inch, in the sand. I could hear the sound of my own grunting combine with the rhythmic squish of the ground giving way under the wheels of the bicycle and felt seized by a strange terror at the idea that we'd be so nakedly seen. My wife, now framed by the ocean and suddenly very far away, never stopped running.

I'M TAKING TOO LONG HERE getting to the part of the story I want to tell. I suppose I've been delaying it. It's a bad habit. But there is a balance to things that can't be upset. When I was young, I stole from my friends, my understanding parents, everybody. I'd get caught, and eventually I quit, but the feeling carries, the thrill and deep shame of it. I was a fearful kid. Everything I loved, I kept for myself. If you are the sort of person who keeps secrets, it's not a habit easily shed.

After we had dinner that night, we came home early. We fell into bed. My wife tossed and turned, and finally turned her back to me, as was her habit when sleeping. I listened as her breathing flattened out and gained the percussive musicality of sleep I'd grown accustomed to. I loved her, I knew that. That was not in doubt. And she loved me. But sadness had been predicted for us. And sadness accrues. It was circling us, growing, getting closer.

I must have fallen asleep, for I have no idea what time it was when I left the bed. By the quality of the darkness I knew that it was late. I stood, unable to see, near the door to our room. Because, I think, the room did not appear to me to be recognizable, I could not prevent myself from swaying. I looked at my wife. She was trying to tell me something in sleep. I stayed there for who knows how long. She faced the wall.

I don't know what compelled me to dress and leave the room. The hallway was lit. Sometimes that's enough. I was quiet. I passed a wall of photographs. I walked softly down the stairs, keeping my steps close to the bannister to avoid creaking the house awake. And there I stood in the blazing foyer, unsure of what to do next, or where to go. The house, to me, suddenly felt immense. I knew it was not true, but I could not shake the suspicion that I could not find my way back to my room, and to my wife, if I had tried. I was torn between the panic of wanting to return, and the calmness of knowing that if I simply stayed here, in the foyer, I would eventually be found.

Can I tell you how long I stayed there? I cannot. I heard a number of cars go by. I heard the rustle of the trees just

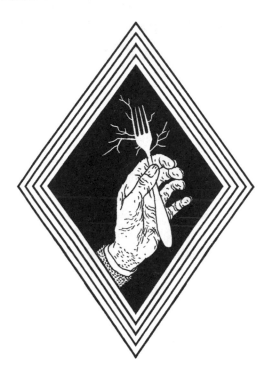

outside the front door. I heard a branch draw a wind-blown, high-pitched circle on one of the windowpanes.

The kitchen was hung with garlic knots and decorative plates. There was an immense wooden table. I was a kid again. I moved around that kitchen, looking for something. I opened all the cupboards. I opened and closed the door to the stove. I felt like the house was whispering against me, urging me back to my own room, but I fought against it. In one drawer, near the sink, I found some old photographs. In another, just below, was the silver. And then I found what I was looking for—when I saw it, I knew its radiant power—and I wrapped it in a napkin, tucked it under my sweatshirt, and made my way back upstairs.

THE NEXT FEW DAYS were soggy, and gray, the kind of weather we'd come for. We stayed in our room, listening to the rain pit the roof. One afternoon we slipped across the street to the Anglican church, where we met a small group of elderly congregants. They treated us as if we were visiting dignitaries come to tell them about the Great American Midwest. It didn't matter to them that we had met, initially, in New York. They wanted to hear about snow. Our bags were still delayed. We bought paperbacks and read them in the Laundromat as the clothes we did have thumped around.

We ate breakfast in pubs, walked on the shore. And nightly I was visited by an apparition of M.—sometimes in the shape of a bird, sometimes as a shadow figure pinned to the ceiling above me—that followed me into the deepest sleep. Give it back, give it back, he was saying. We stood on the edge of a building, overlooking a town I had never seen. Give it back, he said, his wings flapping close to my ear. He followed me home. I was in my mother's arms and she was singing to me. I was on my father's shoulders, as he walked up a flight of stairs. I am the bringer of death. Give it back, he said. But I was no longer afraid.

WE COULD HAVE LEFT—I could've suggested it, I could've insisted—but we had paid for the week and were almost out of money. I didn't tell my wife about my dreams, I just slid into the bed next to her. She moved to me, curled as a ball. Each night I told myself I would explain everything to her in the morning, that I'd done what I did for her, because her story had compelled me to do it, but when the morning came, I forgot. I told myself that if we saw M. again, I would tell her I didn't understand it myself, but we didn't run into M. again, not in any meaningful way. I told myself that if M. ever found me out, I'd return what I'd taken, and pay for a second week we wouldn't use. But he didn't. We adjusted to the time change, our bodies caught up with us. Our bags arrived. We made love, a confirmation, a suture, call it what you will. The pendulum had swung in our favor. We were full of life, a surprise, an embarrassment, and had plenty of it to give.

Our last night, after dinner, we found ourselves still unaccountably hungry. We went down the road to a restaurant. Who knows why it was open? It was 10 p.m. by the time we were seated. And what a feast! We ate pickled herring, bread, apple skewers; pork scratchings with mustard dipping sauce; oysters with apple foam topped with ham; mussels and chives served in a chowder, hand-poured at the table; crab risotto; cured pork; smoked wigeon with quince and a light mustard foam sauce; sturgeon with seaweed and greens; breaded lamb stomach with mint leaf sauce; cream cheese ice cream with pear puree; and finally a nutmeg-coated tartlet, which, when I thought no one was looking, I just licked and returned to my plate. The hanging lanterns inside the restaurant blazed with a light so warm and bright I thought to myself that whatever fires lit this most holy of spaces, they must never go out.

In the morning, we left our keys on the bed as instructed and walked right out. M. was nowhere to be found. I pulled the car around for one final sweep, a goodbye to the house, and as we passed the front, I looked up and there he was, standing in the window, mouthing something I couldn't make out, his hands moving like little birds, flitting around, stitching the air, unwilling to land.

As the plane banked, New York came through the small port window like the idea of industry, a huge hulking land where everyone worked. Another bank and the buildings sprang into full view: the place where we'd met, the land of eternal happiness. The city would always be that way because we had left it behind and would never be back. Forget your dreams, you might say, you have said. But all of this happened; we were happy for a while. And M. That poor man. That hideous soul! Though I tell no one, I think of him frequently. I'm sure he's dead now. He died so that my son, a child who greeted the world with indiscriminate love, who was incandescent at birth, now a young man in possession of his own stories and a light he no longer shares with us, could live.

FABLE
\\\\\\\

IT WAS SATURDAY NIGHT and the four of them were sitting around the dining room table at Sasha's house, telling stories. *Do you remember, do you remember?*—that was the song they were singing. Nils and Anna hadn't seen Sasha for years—they'd missed the wedding, and didn't know Karen, his third wife, at all. But there were no hard feelings; they drank, had some mood-loosening hash; it was like no time had passed. At dinner, Sasha had clapped and rubbed his hands together, blown through his fingers as though he were holding dice. He'd sung of the friends they'd had in common and spoke of their great adventures. He'd told the stories of their youth in such luxurious and precise detail that the episodes began to seem new, as if they'd happened to someone else.

Dinner had been delicious, ram and ewe, heaping platters of food. Now they were into the wine, and it seemed no one wanted the night to end. At some point, Karen stood and wandered around the kitchen, where she spent half an hour opening and closing drawers as Sasha held forth. "I feel like a sultan," Sasha said. "This is Homeric. We're riding the lightning here. Pass the lute, for this has been the best night yet." He reached for his cup and began talking again.

"He never listens," Karen said from the kitchen. She had the refrigerator open and was staring into its gray light as though it held some sort of secret scroll.

"Have mercy," Sasha said, and clutched at his heart.

THE HOUSE WAS DEEP in the country, and it had taken Anna and Nils almost an hour of driving narrow, winding roads to find it. When Nils had tried to apologize for being late—trouble with the kids, a new babysitter—he'd been waved off. "Old friends," Sasha said, wrapping him in a bear hug so tight his neck hurt. "And Anna, still so beautiful. Welcome." He'd made them little paper hats, which he placed on their heads as they stepped through the door. "Remember these?" he'd said. "Of course," said Anna. It was something he'd done when they were in grad school. Each hat, when unfolded, revealed some sort of blessing or fortune you would take with you into the good, cool night. It was, in fact, how Nils and Anna had met.

"I see you've got your hats," Karen said.

"We're playing along," Anna said.

Nils folded his and put it in his jacket pocket.

"Fine, fine, you don't have to look now," Sasha said. "Save it for the drive home. But don't forget. Or it'll never come true." He shut the door and began pouring drinks. This was how things had always gone between the three of them. They took themselves to the dining room, and the night unfurled like a dark sail around them.

KAREN RETURNED TO THE TABLE as Sasha was winding down. With some shock, Nils and Anna had come to realize that a number of the old friends they'd been talking about—not close friends, but still—were now dead: one or two heart attacks, a ski accident, cancer. A great spin on the roulette wheel, the marble magnetized, succinct, final. Sasha pushed out his chair and walked down the hall to the bathroom. "It's unendurable," he said when he came back. His cheeks were flushed, and Anna thought he might've been crying. "They stand on the banks," he said. "They're in this very room." A thick, heavy silence fell over the group. As though recounting a dream, Sasha then began to list his own reversals in fortune, which had been great—he'd built and lost companies, an accident had left him unable to have children—and what he had learned from them, which was almost nothing. "Except for this: if you find a beautiful woman, you hang on, you hang on, you hang on," he said, looking at Karen, "and you never let go."

The effect that these stories had on Nils and Anna was immediate and strange. As their old friend spoke, each scene, familiar and not, had emerged as though from some shrouded, timeless woods, taken physical shape on the table in front of them, and said: study me for the clues to your life. And what did they see? Only that they, themselves, had been lucky, happy; they'd been content. They were not dead, they'd had their children. There was nothing wrong with celebrating that, but that's not what stories were supposed to do, and the idea that they'd arrived at some point where all had been said was, somehow, horrendous. Who would want that?

Karen reached out and rested her hand on the crook of Sasha's elbow. Anna and Nils reluctantly folded their napkins. Outside, the wind picked up and blew little gusts of snow against the kitchen window, and for a minute it seemed as though no one would ever speak again.

"Karen tells stories," Sasha finally said. He coughed into his hand. "It's what she does for a living."

"Translates," Karen said.

"Really?" Anna said. "I didn't know that."

"Why would you? I'm the odd man out."

"We haven't asked you a single question," Nils said. "We've been rude."

"She's incredibly smart," Sasha said. "You, I mean. You are incredibly smart."

Anna turned to Karen. "Perhaps you could tell us a love story," she said.

"Yes," said Nils, and patted her hand. "If you have one, it's the best way to end."

"They aren't really love stories," Karen said. "They're more like fables."

"Surprise us," Sasha said. "We can switch gears. I think that's something we're ready for."

They cleared the table, and took themselves to the spacious living room, where they sat on an L-shaped couch that faced an enormous gas fireplace.

"This is our first time out in who knows how long," Anna said. She sat close to Nils on the couch. The night was approaching its natural end, of course, but Anna felt as though something important was on the verge of passing between her and Nils, and in that sense the evening didn't feel finished. She took his hand. Their babysitter would be wondering where they were, but she knew to call if something was wrong.

Karen returned from her office with a stack of loose paper, which she arranged messily on her lap. She read silently for a few minutes and no one said a word. "This one," she finally said, "is new. It doesn't fit with what you were talking about earlier." She rubbed her belly with an open palm. She was frowning slightly. "But it's been bothering me, and I'd like to try it out."

"Is it a love story at all?" Anna said. "Will we be scared?"

"Yes," Karen said. "No. It's about a forest, and two foxes, and a wolf." She hesitated. "And a woman," she finally said. "You might find it upsetting because you have children. But it *is* about love. It begins as a love story, but it becomes something else, too."

"Okay," Sasha said. He was fiddling with the fire. He couldn't get it to work, and there was a brief silence as

Karen regarded him. He quit fumbling and sat down. Then she began.

"ONCE UPON A TIME," she said, "in a tall, thick forest that grew next to a northern village, a small fox lived with his wife. For many years they'd been content, their days together long and full. But when it came time to have a child, and they found they could not—for each child they conceived arrived stillborn, some fur but no breath, and left a stain of blood upon the snow—they were visited by great sadness. Over time this sadness bloomed a shadow, and soon grief hung on their door. The forest fell dark, the nights became long, and the joy they'd previously felt in each other's company could no longer be found. Days passed with no words of comfort. When, at night, they reached for each other, it was like touching air. *This cannot go on*, thought the fox. And so, one day he left his tired wife sleeping and returned only as the sun was going down with a human child they could call their own.

"His wife met him at the door. He handed the bundle to her as though it were a great gift, and the small child seemed to glow in her arms. He cried softly, he cuddled, he burrowed directly into his wife's neck. He was unafraid. She let out one happy sob and brought the swaddled child inside. That night, they fed him milk and meat, poured water from a basin, bathed him with their tongues. He grabbed playfully for their bristly fur. They made a bed out of branches and sang him asleep in a tidy corner of their den.

"In bed that first night, she reached for her husband. I didn't know what I'd do, she said quietly. Before long, she stole from their bed and returned with the sleeping child in her arms. They listened to the wind outside. It began as a whisper, then grew louder and more fulsome. Boughs cracked and fell. Then it stopped, and it seemed the forest was as quiet as it had ever been.

"In the morning, the child stirred, stretched, and opened his eyes. Welcome, she said. We have been waiting for you our entire lives, and we have so much to tell you."

KAREN CLEARED HER THROAT. "However," she said, "bringing this child into their home did not come without complication. For in doing so the fox had broken the oldest rule in the forest, which was this: the separation between the village and woods must always be maintained. This meant that no matter how happy they were, they would always have to hide this child. Any transgression, even a slight breaking of this rule, meant death."

"By whom?" Anna said.

"Wolf," Karen said. "He patrolled the woods and kept its boundary. He'd been around in one shape or another for a long time, and killed whomever he pleased, including, years ago, the fox's father. And the second complication was this," she continued. "The fox had not found the small child by the river, abandoned for the nuns, as he had told his wife. He'd stolen him from a small house near the edge of the forest. This was not an impulse. He'd watched for weeks from the woods. He'd heard the child's cry, seen

his mother soothe him, and waited patiently until one day, as he knew she would, the woman left her child alone on a blanket on the porch. The fox didn't hesitate. He slipped on his father's magic cloak, took on the form of an old man, and, breaking the rule, stepped quickly out of the forest. As he ran away with the child in his arms, he heard the woman calling for him; her cries were like the screaming wind. It was the most desolate sound imaginable."

Here Karen paused. Sasha had started fiddling with the fireplace again.

"He'd taken the child and left the woman, who had no one else, no husband, no parents, all alone," she said. "But he thought: what is her unhappiness, compared to ours? This was something he could never tell his wife, for she was kind and knew something of loneliness, and would not forgive him for his cruelty."

THE CHILD GREW QUICKLY. He learned to turn over, and soon he was sitting by himself. Wherever the fox's wife went, the child followed her with his eyes, and if she was ever out of sight, he balled his fists and cried quietly until she returned to him. Goodness, she'd say, and sweep him into her arms. I'm not going anywhere.

Each morning, the fox woke before the sun, warmed milk on the stove, brought the sleeping child to his wife. Just a little longer, she'd say to him with the child in her arms, and then I will come help you gather wood and wool for the winter. As the sun went down, he'd return to their den in time to hear his wife humming the child to sleep.

They clipped his fingernails, put them in a jar, cleaned the wax from his ears. They bathed him in the brook, sopped the folds of his legs. Gently washed behind his neck, wiped him clean and dry. They sang late into the night. Soon he fell ill with his first fever, and a fearful stillness descended on the home: perhaps, they thought, this was how they'd lose him. But the fox's wife dipped a cloth in cool water, spread it across his uncreased forehead, hushed his cries, and waited for him to return to himself. Soon he did. Now you are ours, she said.

And so their early days as a family passed. They were careful, they kept to themselves. There was no before, only after. They were as dear to each other as could be imagined.

"BUT NOTHING LASTS FOREVER," Karen said, "and soon the weather turned and a sharp feeling began to nag at the fox. He didn't know what it was. Or, he did know— he had lied to his wife, and he dreaded being found out; and he was afraid that Wolf, who had killed his father, would hear of what he'd done and come for him. No one in the forest had seen Wolf in ages; that didn't mean he wasn't there.

"But there was more to it than that. There were days when he spoke to no one, and no one spoke to him; when the child would cry if he held him; when his wife became impatient with him. He felt excluded, and soon began to feel sorry for himself. He wanted to say: you should be grateful for what I've done! I put my life in great danger for your happiness! But then, of course, he would remember that he'd lied to his wife and told her he found the child by the river."

Karen turned a page and continued. "She too noticed the distance growing between them. There's no such thing as too much happiness, she told him one night. She picked up the sleeping child's arm and dropped it gently. Everything else sorts out."

Nils adjusted his legs. It seemed that the couch had grown softer, and now curled around them in the dimly lit room. Anna had her eyes closed. Suddenly, the fire whooshed to life, and Sasha sat down next to Karen. He put his arm around her. "There," he said. In the low firelight, and sitting beside her, he looked older than he had during dinner. "That's better, isn't it?"

"Yes," Karen said. "Much."

WITH WINTER CAME DARKNESS and snow, the sense of an ending, but also the turning and blossoming of something else, and one cold morning the fox wandered a great distance from home. He stepped lightly, followed a path cut by a frozen stream through the woods. He had no destination in mind. Bare branches, encased, glistened with ice. There was no sound that was not muffled, and the gray winter sky felt dense and close.

Soon, and for reasons he couldn't understand, he began to feel light-headed. He paused to catch his breath. Suddenly, he had a vision of the forest from a great height, as though he soared above it. He shook his head. Next, he smelled summer grasses, though they were buried in snow. *This is strange*, he thought. *I must be very tired.* He found a small hollow under a great oak tree and soon fell into a deep sleep in which he dreamed he was wandering the forest, looking for a handful of berries he'd lost. Then he dreamed of his wife before their child—he saw her in bed, waiting for him. His body began to quiver. It was not a dream he wanted to end. But soon the image of his wife began to drip at its edges, and he felt fear rise in his throat. His wife gave way to a vision of Wolf, lurking in the forest, watching him with his viscous, yellow eyes. He could smell Wolf's decaying breath. His father was there.

WHEN HE WOKE, it was to the sound of anxious chirping. *What have I done?* he thought. When he arrived home, his wife met him at the door. Where were you? she said. I was worried. Nowhere, he said. Well, she said, we have news.

With this she stepped aside. The child sat in the middle of the floor. Then, with one chubby arm, he reached for a stool, pulled himself standing, and began to take his first steps.

He's been working all day just to show you, his wife said. She was beaming.

The fox knew it wasn't true, and that she'd said it only to include him. She rested her head on his shoulder.

He will want to go outside, the fox finally said. It's too dangerous.

I know, his wife said. I've thought of that.

She stood and retrieved a child-sized vest she had sewn from the fox's own cloak, and with a flourish she draped it gently across the child's shoulders. Now, rather than a human child holding on to the stool, there appeared a small fox. *My father would not have liked this*, the fox thought. Then he said so to his wife.

Your father isn't here, she said. And no one will ever know.

"THE CHILD GREW," said Karen. "His hair was black and knotted, his eyes were like little dark stones. He was sweet-natured, curious about every little thing." She coughed and adjusted the pages in front of her. "Every morning, before leaving their den, they dressed him in his vest, and every night upon returning they hung it near the fire to dry. They were wary of the magic contained in this cloak, but it allowed them to leave their den, and with the child appearing to all like a fox, perhaps they wouldn't even warrant a second glance. The child clung to the fox's back, and they ran through the cold in the falling snow. They trotted, they gamboled, they hunted together. The forest in winter was beautiful, and there were mornings where it felt to the fox and his wife as if the trees and sky and rolling hills, the blue-lit afternoons and evenings, had been created for them alone.

"But still there were some nights the fox could not sleep, and on those nights he found himself wondering about the child's real mother. Sometimes she appeared to him in his dreams, walking through the forest, calling for her child, heartbroken, bereft. In these dreams, she moved through the woods, looking behind every tree, in every den. Other times he imagined her as a pale, long-fingered ghost who came into the forest not to find her child but to kill whomever had taken him. She moved like the wind; she would not stop. Often, he'd wake just as she had found them, and he would go and stand at the door and listen to the night sounds in the forest until he calmed down.

"This small, small child," Karen continued. "His wife could not be without him, nor he without her. He would not eat unless it was she offering food. When the fox held him, singing, he would not sleep until his wife gently took him back into her arms. Time passed; they were content.

But one night, looking directly at the ceiling while his wife slept, he thought: she is wrong, there is such a thing as too much happiness. If it announces itself too garishly, someone will come to snatch it away."

SASHA STOOD UP to get a drink.

"What do you do with a story like this?" Nils asked. "When you're done, I mean."

"I suppose that when I have enough of them, I'll put them all together and make a book."

"I read these stories when I was a kid," Anna said. "I couldn't get enough."

"Right," said Karen.

"I'm back," announced Sasha, and sat down near Nils.

"So," Karen said, and looked down at the pages in front of her. "He can't stop thinking about this woman, the child's mother. There are some days when, for reasons he can't quite explain, she enters his every waking thought. It's alarming to him, and unexpected. He doesn't know what to do."

"Right," Sasha said. "We got that."

"No," Karen said, "like, he *really* thinks about her." She stopped here and looked at Anna. "This isn't a children's story. It's something else."

"I'm sorry," Anna said. "I didn't mean to upset you. Excuse me," she said, and stood. She walked down the hall to the bathroom. While she was gone, no one spoke. The fire was blue at its base, and licked the fake logs in a hypnotic, predictable way. When Anna returned, she sat near the edge of the sofa, close to, but not touching, her husband.

"Where were we?" Karen said. She looked at the page in front of her for where she'd left off.

"He's thinking about the woman," Nils said. "The child's mother."

"Yes," Karen said. "Right. Time passed, and this unsettled feeling did not go away. It felt to the fox as though the woman were reaching out to him across some other plane, some dark dimension he couldn't quite see. He was deeply bothered by this feeling. It would not let him go. And so one day, even though he knew it was not a great idea, he left home and went in search of her."

THOUGH HE KNEW WHERE the woman lived, the fox was apprehensive about returning. He walked for most of the day and then paused at the edge of the woods. With a backwards glance, he drew the cloak over his shoulders. He felt the transformation in his chest, painful but quick.

The child's house was as he remembered: red door, peeling shutters. The garden grew untended and wild. Dry sticks lay across the brittle lawn and he was careful with his steps as he approached.

It appeared that no one was home. He looked in one window, then another. He saw the woman's bed was unmade. The kitchen smelled of rotting food. The child's room was untouched, as though he were expected back at any moment.

Then he saw her: thin and dressed in her nightclothes, she sat alone in front of the fireplace. He couldn't see her face. He cupped his hands to the window, and then, as if she knew he was there, she stood and made her way across the room. She moved slowly and gracefully, walked as though she were the ghost he'd seen in his dreams. *Leave*, his thoughts commanded him, but he could not. She pulled at him with a strange gravity, and he found himself wanting to speak to her. Her hair was matted and snarled, the hem of her nightgown stained with mud. She *had* been in the forest, after all.

He retreated to the woods until night fell. He tried to clear his head but could not: it felt as though his brain had become gauze. When it was dark he returned, stood by her window, and watched as she lay down in her empty bed, closed her eyes, and slept. He did not know what to do. Finally, he wrapped the cloak around his shoulders, climbed through the window, and slipped into the bed next to her. She smelled like an animal at the end of its life. Her very breath was sorrow. Even in sleep she must've known he was not her child, but nonetheless she curled around him, pulled him to the hollow of her rancid chest, and fell into a deeper dream, the deepest there was. She called to her child, wanting only him. He remained in her embrace and listened.

Finally, he pulled away. He left through the window, closed it, and swept his footprints from the garden's bed. On the front porch, he left the child's blanket, and on top of that a pile of small bones. It would hurt at first, he knew, but it was better this way.

"TIME PASSED AND THE FOX JUST . . . did nothing," Karen said. "Now and then he returned to the house and lay with the woman, but that soon stopped, and soon he found he could live with the pain he'd caused, and the lie he'd told his wife, simply by pretending he hadn't done anything wrong. In fact, it was a secret he liked keeping. Occasionally, a vision of the woman haunted him, but mostly she didn't, and the fox family lived happily for a while. They kept to themselves, but their old friends understood, and soon stopped visiting. All families turn inward over time. It is what happens when a child arrives. Habits are broken, and new habits are formed, clung to. It's one of the old stories. It's how you stay safe."

There was a loud sound from the kitchen, followed by a rush of water. "That's just the dishwasher," Sasha said. "It's a piece of garbage."

"Anyway," Karen continued, "soon the leaves began to change and the days grew cold and short, and the fox, in his state of contentedness, forgot about the woman in the village and what he'd done. But one winter morning he woke early and knew something wasn't right: the forest was a little too quiet, the sun late in rising. He crept out of bed and went outside. When it should have been light, it was dark. Where he should've smelled a crisp winter morning, he smelled something animal and foul. He blinked his eyes and swatted at his nose to clear the stench. And when he looked up, he saw that Wolf had come, and now sat near his door.

"Wolf was enormous and lanky. He moved rarely, and only when he felt like it. His eyes were yellow and depthless, unblinking; he thought in a slow and deliberate way. The fox hadn't seen him in years, and he felt his stomach drop in fear.

"*It's so strange*, Wolf finally said. *A human in the woods.*

What is she looking for, I wonder? The fox shook his head. He could not speak. *I know you've seen her,* Wolf said. *And I know where you go at night.* Then he stood. His mouth was a black gaping pit. *It's not something we can have,* he finally said. *It just isn't.*

"The fox felt urine stream down his rooted leg. He was remembering his father. He closed his eyes and prepared for his own life to end. But when it didn't, he slowly uncovered his head. He opened his eyes and with relief realized that Wolf hadn't mentioned his wife or the child. He nodded at Wolf and said he would not see the woman again. At this, Wolf laughed. And then he opened his mouth and commenced with a great yawn. *We'll see,* he said. And with that, he turned and walked slowly back into the forest."

"Hmm," Sasha said. "That was easy."

"No, no," Karen said. "A visit from Wolf is never that simple."

THAT MORNING WHEN THE CHILD WOKE, he was unhappy and listless, wan, full of complaint. Soon, he caught a cold and slept for two days. When he woke, it was like something inside him had shifted; as though the little machine of his heart fluttered here and there irregularly, and as a result different chords were pulled in his mind, and the song he sang changed its key. Some days, he was content to play on his own. Other days he was inconsolable. On these days, the fox could feel his wife's sadness returning. It was like a low fog sifting over the forest floor, pushing at the windows of their den, trying to get in. Month after month passed, and they became exhausted, short with one another, angry themselves.

If the child cried for more than a day, sometimes the fox's wife took the cloak from its peg and transformed into a young woman. Her paws became fingers, her brown eyes turned blue. From the door she would glide to wherever the child was and take him in her arms, sing softly, wipe his tears with her thumb. This always calmed him. And once he was asleep, she would remove the cloak, lie down next to her husband, and quietly weep on his shoulder.

"FOR MONTHS," KAREN SAID, "this sadness afflicted them. They began to feel . . . helpless. There was nothing to be done. The forest was heavy with snow, the light was flat. The child wanted nothing to do with either of them. He sat cross-legged in a corner, stared at the wall. He walked in small circles in the center of the room. When picked up, he thrashed and screamed. Sometimes he would cry for hours, and the crying would make him vomit. He stopped eating.

"And then one day," Karen said, "they woke up and the child was gone." She paused. "They looked everywhere," she finally said. "They had not left their door open, and the child could not unlatch it. There were no windows left ajar. A child like that could not just disappear, but that seemed to be exactly what had happened. For a week they walked the woods, calling his name. They left the door open at night in the hope that he would return on his own, left food in places around the forest, they begged and cried and prayed, but he didn't return. Soon a winter storm arrived. The temperature dropped, and the wind picked up, and the forest floor was covered even more deeply with snow. It was the worst storm they'd seen in years. Neither would say it, but they knew all hope of finding the child was lost. Soon, his wife took to their bed and would not leave it. When the fox tried to talk to her, to reassure her, it was like talking to an empty box. She'd gone vacant. When he brought her food, it remained uneaten."

Karen cleared her throat. "When the storm relented, he left her and resumed his search in the woods. He crossed the stream and traveled farther than he ever had, to the darkest parts of the forest, asking everyone he met about the human child. The answer was always the same. He knew the woman had not found and taken the child back—every night he ventured to her house to peer into her windows. She sat alone in her living room, staring into whatever dark space unfurled in front of her. The child had not returned."

"He just disappeared?" Sasha said.

"You need to stop interrupting," Karen said, and looked at him with what appeared, to Anna and Nils, to be genuine anger. "The three of you have been talking all night," she said, "You asked for a story, it's almost done."

"Sorry," Nils said,

"Yes," said Anna, "please continue."

EVENTUALLY, WITH HIS WIFE still sick in bed, the fox went in search of Wolf. After two days of walking and

calling for the child even though he knew all hope was lost, the forest opened, and he found Wolf standing at the mouth of a great cave. Near the entrance, blanched and cracked skulls were heaped like stones. Enormous worms wound around his paws. Wolf nodded to the fox. He grinned, then dropped his head and returned to licking the pile of bones at his feet. *I have*, he said, *no idea why you've come.*

The fox was struck dumb. The darkness that orbited Wolf stretched its living fingers and beckoned to him. But then he felt anger surging from his shoulders like an old thought. He crossed the distance between them and lunged.

Oh, ho! said Wolf, surprised and even slightly pleased at the fox's stupidity. He bit again and again at Wolf's neck while Wolf stood to his full height and did nothing at all. The fox felt the large worms wrap around him. They squeezed his legs, his hips, his chest. *Your pain is the breaking of the shell that encloses your understanding,*

Wolf finally said. *Tell me when you are tired, and then I will show you something.* Eventually, the fox could no longer stand, and with great heaving gulps of air lay down. With a yawn, Wolf turned and stepped into his cave without a backward look.

The fox felt as though he'd left the earth. He no longer cared about anything at all. The walls of the cave were wet and putrid, and as he followed Wolf, the sounds of the forest receded behind him. It was as though he were slowly entering a cold and unforgiving afterlife. With some sadness, he realized his memories of his own father had been wiped clean: when he tried to think of him now, he saw only a dark and bending absence. Finally, the tunnel opened up to a great cavern, lit by torches. He was met by the smell of decomposing leaves. There was no sound at all. The floor was piled high with bones. *You see?* Wolf said, and shrugged. *There are no children here.*

KAREN ADJUSTED HERSELF on the couch and looked quickly around the room.

"His wife did not recover. In the morning he brought her tea, breakfast. She refused to eat. She refused to leave the bed. She refused to allow him to move the child's belongings—the cloak she'd made, the toys. His clothes. In the evening, he crawled next to her and sometimes it was like sleeping with a statue. Other times, she talked in her sleep, thrashed, and nested; she roamed her own unconscious, dark roads that did not end. One night, she opened her eyes, looked directly at her husband, and said: That's not true. The fox didn't know to what she was referring. He knew that he had brought her great pain, but he had not said anything for days.

"And so they moved carefully through the fraught and fragile months. They searched the forest out of habit. They took no pleasure in the passing hours. During the first year, the child visited them both in their sleep, and in these dream visions the fox saw a young man standing near the edge of the forest, one arm raised in greeting. His wife saw him running through the woods, with sunlight at his back. Neither saw him for what he was.

"As time passed, the fox found he could no longer remember what the child looked like. When he tried to imagine him, all he saw was a large white stone that gave off a shimmering light and vibrated with hatred for him and what he'd done. His wife remembered, though. She could describe the child's chubby legs, and the constellation of his birthmarks, his thick black hair, the feel of his toothless gums on her outstretched wrist. His smell. She removed the cloak from its peg, transformed into a woman, and sat in the middle of the room for days as if to call him back. But it was for naught. The boy, the fox felt, no longer existed, and after his disappearance they'd invented and replaced him with a different child made from memory— it was this they were mourning, and warming themselves by. It was not enough, but it was what they had."

"And so," Karen said, "that was how they aged."

"And he never tells her," Anna said. "Not about Wolf, not about the woman, not about the child."

"Well," Karen said. "It's complicated. One of the things

he'd seen in the cave were the small bones of their still-born children. So he was shaken, and he tried hard to forget that, and did his best to keep that knowledge from his wife. If you keep one secret, you can't tell another—eventually all of it will come out. Many years passed, however," she said. "And finally, when they were old and near death themselves, and all of this was a distant memory, and perhaps he thought he'd be forgiven, the fox confessed to what he'd done. He began on the day he brought the child home, and he told her about the woman, and his visits to her house, and how, one spring morning, he'd opened the door and seen Wolf. She listened patiently. Her face made no expression he recognized. He felt unburdened, like a weight was off his neck and shoulders; but he also felt deep shame at the way he had kept this from her. She did not rescue him from this feeling."

"Good," said Anna. "That seems about right."

THE NEXT DAY, he woke to an empty bed. He sat up and saw she'd cleaned their den. Everything was in its place: the floor swept, the child's toys tucked neatly in the corner, the clothes she'd sewn for him years ago folded and stacked. She stood near the fire. Take me to her, she instructed her husband. She opened the door and stepped out.

By the time they got to the village, the sun was going down and the sky was gold-streaked and orange. They shared the cloak, now old and moth-bitten, and felt the quickening of their transformation: a short old woman and a fat, ugly old man, shuffling together, arm-in-arm. No one paid them any mind. They passed husbands, wives, children; through open windows they heard dinner conversations, spoons on plates, the sounds of family happiness. Finally, they reached the house they were looking for. It was as he remembered it.

The woman answered. She'd had little company over the years, and her face betrayed neither shock nor recognition at the sight of this odd couple at her door. She was polite and invited them in. She led them through the small house, and they sat facing one another in ratty and dirty chairs as the sky dimmed, banded blue, then went dark.

I'd offer you tea, but I have none, the woman finally said. She was old now. Her features were like carved wood, and her eyes were as dark as night. She studied them closely, violently cleared her throat, and resumed staring.

I've been waiting for you, she finally said, and I know why you're here. Then she said the child's name. The fox's wife began to cry. Are you here to bring him back? the woman asked.

When neither the fox nor his wife spoke, she had her answer. She sighed and looked out the window. She composed herself and dabbed at her cheeks with a large square of blue cloth. The fox recognized it as the blanket he'd left on her doorstep years ago.

Finally, the fox felt his wife tug at the cloak, and saw the woman startle at their change in appearance.

His wife spoke first. She described their den in the forest, the light of the seasons, where they lived and how. She described how they'd made the child's bed, taught him to run and burrow and hide. She talked of the long nights when he had a fever and the relief she felt when it broke.

The woman listened closely. Was he very happy? she finally said. Did he sleep through the night? Did he pull his ear to soothe himself like he used to?

This is some sort of trap, the fox thought. He tried to look for her teeth, to see if she'd sharpened them, but she kept them well hidden, and he found that he could answer these questions, and that talking like this settled his mind. The woman leaned forward in her chair.

You've brought him back to me, she said.

No, the fox's wife said, and let out a soft cry. No, we haven't. He's gone.

The woman spread her arms.

You've brought him back, she said. She seemed to grow in her seat. It was the not knowing, she said. It was imagining the darkness, and his pain. That's what it was. That's all it is. This is the end of your life. That's all it could ever be.

And then she wept too.

"AND THAT'S THE END?" Sasha said.

"Yes," Karen said.

"They just cry?" said Nils.

"Well, there's another version," said Karen, "in which there is no reunion. And another version, where the woman reaches for the fox and squeezes him to death with her bare hands for what he did. And a third version, where the child returns, now a man." Karen was sweating slightly. She seemed relieved to finally put the story down, ready to go to bed. She had one hand on her belly and rubbed it as though it might bring her luck. "The three of you. You should see your faces," she said. "Do you want to hear what Wolf originally said? It's an old poem. He said: *Your pain is the breaking of the shell that encloses your understanding. And could you keep your heart in wonder at the daily miracles of your life, your pain would not seem less wondrous than your joy. Pain is the bitter potion by which the physician within you heals your sick self. Trust the physician and drink his remedy in silence and tranquility.* I didn't include that this time, though. Even though I like it."

"Huh," Sasha said.

Karen was looking out the window now. "This is the end of your life," she said.

IT WAS LATE. The fable had taken them long into the night, and there would be no more stories. Anna and Nils knew their babysitter was most likely asleep on their couch, the television quiet and casting a blue light across her tranquil, young face. For a long time no one moved, and the four of them sat as though rooted to the couch. To someone standing outside the house, peering in, they would've appeared as a still life in which each solitary figure was lost in thought, flat-lipped, as though on the verge of hearing the answer to some private riddle. But of course, they had heard the answer. Finally, someone coughed and the spell was broken.

"Did you ever open your hats?" Sasha said.

"We didn't," said Nils. "I forgot mine completely."

A young snow began pelting the roof. They would need to leave soon; they should've left hours ago. Perhaps now, Anna thought, they would never leave. But just then, there was a thunderous *crack*, and the lights in the kitchen cut out. The fire sputtered, hissed, and went out as well, and the room was plunged into complete darkness.

"Here's the scary story you were asking for," Sasha said. He stood. "We've got candles somewhere."

"Don't bother," Nils said. "Our eyes will adjust." But Sasha was already knocking into furniture as he crossed the room.

"I liked that story," Anna said. "Very much."

"Thank you," Karen said.

Nils reached for his wife in the darkness, but when he grasped, he felt nothing but air. Had she moved? He heard noise from the kitchen, cabinets being open and shut. It sounded like an animal was rooting around. "Anna," he said, but she didn't answer. Finally, he saw her and was struck by a pale fear, though he didn't know why. She had stood and was at the window. "Anna," he said again, but she was thinking of something else. An image had come to her: their first child, in her arms, in the early morning, both of them lost in those tired happy days that never seemed to end but could not be remembered, and would not come again.

"I've got one," Sasha said from the kitchen. "I've found a candle. Hang on, hang on, hang on. Nobody move. Soon there will be light. Nobody move a muscle. I'll be right there."

They waited, but he never came.

ANGUS AND ANNABEL

\\\\\\\\\

IT WAS DARK NOW and the night birds sang. Angus heard their calls through his bedroom window and wished them gone. Annabel stirred in the bed next to him, kicked, but didn't wake. For the last four days she'd been unwell. Tonight, he'd lain with her in their small room until she quieted, listened as her breathing became regular and she lost rigidity to sleep. He imagined her mind at rest, a leniency. She was nine years old, younger than he by three years.

These birds—their music was anxious and obscure, songs of distance heralding distance. Eventually they quelled and silence descended. He listened to the fire in the next room, the soft push of air, and fixed his eyes on the low ceiling above them. Now his sister's grip loosened and her arm, pressed to his, became slack and heavy. It was just the two of them in the house. Their mother was dead, their father would be returning soon.

He left the bed and made his way out of their room. He fed a log to the dimming fire, laced his boots. He stopped at the front door and listened for any sound from where his sister lay. Hearing none, he lifted the latch and let himself outside.

It was late September, the temperature on the verge of plunging. From where he stood, Angus could clearly see where the cut grass of their property gave way to thicker growth, the dark silhouette of closer trees against the perfect black of the forest behind. A young moon hung low in the sky. Inside, the darkness of these nights was flat, without depth—it encroached and pushed at the windows, asking to be let in. But outside, the dark had quality, a palette and texture of its own.

It was the elm—the one in their yard, their mother's tree—that had upset his sister. He could see it now, a whorl in the darkness, its branches bending gently in the wind. Tonight, when her fit started, she'd pointed to the window and said the tree had been reaching for them. Angus had not seen this. He'd tried to calm her, but she wouldn't be calmed. This was the tree their mother had loved and named, decorated in the spring when she was still herself. The decorations were gone now—their father, in his anger and grief, had seen to it—but the thick tree still stood. Its trunk was too large for the two of them, holding hands, to circle. They touched it gently when they thought no one was looking. He'd seen his sister lean her forehead on its rough bark on her way to the barn.

Now, near the door of their house, he stood motionless, daring the tree to show him something, fearful it might. The wind moved through the leaves with a sound like creek water. An image of their mother and the doctor came to him, and he tried to push it from his mind. To remember is to call forth, he thought.

Earlier, when his sister's fit had begun, he'd cradled her to prevent her head from hitting the floor with too much force; and when he'd taken her to their room, he'd been careful not to disturb her. He knew his presence helped. If he were not next to her, in the bed they shared, her kicking would not stop. She would cry out and speak of things he could make no sense of. He could not guess where the danger to her came from, or how it began; its arrival was sudden. Over the last few days, as these visions had come to her, rooted, and left, they thought only of their mother and what their father had done. She'd had no fever. Now, to recover, his sister would place her hand in his, a cold grip, and press her head firmly to her pillow as if willing herself still. He pulled her close, whispered comfort in her ear. He smoothed her sweat-stiffened hair. It'll pass, he said. Be patient. It'll pass.

And it did pass. In the mornings, she was herself. But tomorrow their father would return and they would have to be even more careful.

He watched the woods until the cold drove him back inside. He would lie to his father about the chickens. He'd say foxes or some other animal had bent the wire, scattered the coop. He would not say he'd killed and buried them because they had frightened Annabel and he thought it would help. He didn't know what the punishment would be, but he was resolved to accept it.

He latched the door, made his way past the low fire, hung his coat, and slipped uneasily into the bed next to his sister. She pulled away from him, and he let her.

He could not imagine sleep coming to him, though eventually it did. But before he fell fully he saw his sister. She walked in front of him, just out of reach, hands at her sides, her feet brown with mud. Do not let him see, she'd said earlier as he held her. When he comes back, please, you can't let him see.

WHEN ANGUS WOKE IT WAS EARLY—the morning light pressed flatly through their small bedroom window—and his sister was not in bed. His first thought was that she had left, and his certainty startled him. But where would she go? She was too young to leave without him; they had not been to town for months. He heard sounds from the next room, dressed quickly, and made his way to the kitchen. Annabel sat at the heavy wooden table, still in her bed-clothes. Her brown hair was combed. She wore the white nightgown their mother had sewn—it was fraying at the hem and slightly discolored. She insisted on wearing it when their father was gone. She'd set out two bowls, and when she heard Angus at the door she looked up.

—You slept in your boots, she said.

—I did, Angus said.

—What's to become of us if we sleep in our boots?

She was calm, perhaps still sleepy herself. She was making fun of their father.

—You need to fold that away, Angus said and sat down. He'll be back this afternoon.

—I know, she said. You reminded me last night.

—Did you dream? Angus said.

—I did, but I can't remember, she said. She shifted in her seat and smoothed the nightgown where it had wrinkled.

—What will he do about the chickens? she finally said.

—I don't know, Angus replied and signaled with his hand that the discussion was over.

Their morning routine was set. They finished breakfast and cleaned. Then, in the front room, they sat by the fire. Angus pulled down the one book they owned and handed it to Annabel. He jumped in only when a specific word gave her trouble, or a phrase needed correcting. She spoke with her chin tilted downward, her eyes calmly leveled on the page, lifting only when she was finished with a section, or was proud of working through a passage that had previously given her difficulty. She was small for her age, her thin body a bird's scaffolding. Her reading voice was light and melodic, her dark brown eyes wide and, for now, in this early morning light, unclouded. She furrowed her brow, a model of young concentration. They were no longer schooled but they read every morning. And she was trying. This mimic of studiousness, her effort and care, her desire to remain still—all of this in the light of the morning, gave Angus hope. They would, he thought, get through this together.

OUTSIDE, THE SMELL OF yellowing leaves hung in the air. They walked quietly through the stand of birch trees and passed the pond near the edge of their property. The autumn sun cut mid-sky and shone upon the cold grass. There was no trouble as they picked the apples, no trouble as they passed the elm. Annabel called out the birds as they walked: robin, tree sparrow, grackle, waxwing. Angus cleared the path of sticks. They were working to keep the lines of their property visible, to show their diligence while their father was gone. Their solitude was felt and welcomed and made space for them where they felt none before.

When they reached the small barn, however, his sister stopped, and released his hand. Angus called her name. She didn't respond. He reached for her and she sat down in the grass. He tried to pull her to standing, but she was limp and heavy and would go no further. He stepped away and watched her closely. He was used to this happening at night and had not been wary during the day.

—I'm tired, she said. Don't be angry.

—I'm not angry, he said and shook his head. She studied the ground, cleared it of rocks. She pulled some tall grass and tied the pieces in knots. She moved slowly, but her eyes remained clear. He said her name again. She cleared her throat but didn't speak. Soon she tilted her head toward the sky and sat rigidly alert, as though listening for something Angus could not hear. He knelt next to her, unsure what to do. Soon whatever it had been passed. She sighed. Angus sensed her relief. He stood, and moved behind her, scanned the woods in the light of day until he felt the danger to her was gone for good, and perhaps wasn't coming. He gently stroked the back of her head. Her hair was greasy and brittle. He whispered to her until he felt he could waste no more time.

—Do you want to go back? he said.

—Come with me.

—The cows will be sick. It will only take a minute.

She stood and brushed her coat with her hands. Angus asked if she would be able to manage, and she nodded. He told her he'd follow shortly and watched as she turned up the path and walked slowly to the house. She paused at the elm tree, but she did not touch it. She looked small to him; she was small. He felt a panic rise in his chest but pushed it away. He waited until she was inside before continuing down the path.

The barn was dark and smelled of the earth. The cows

did not greet him, though each leaned toward Angus as he put his hands to their backs. It was only after he'd finished, once he'd pailed the milk and refastened the gate, that he saw the poppets—four of them, set carefully against the inside of the barn door, small sentinels of equal height, no faces, just a knot where the head should be.

Their mother had shown them how to make dolls like this when they were little. They were small stick figurines wrapped in torn pieces of sackcloth. He set down the pail he was carrying, careful not to spill. All sound seemed to leave the barn. He looked over his shoulder and then back to the door. The figures were spread with a foot between them so they covered the beam. He walked slowly over to where they lay and gathered them up. They were light, and hastily made.

As he pulled them apart—first by unwinding the securing twine, then unweaving the small twigs (the cloth he put in his pocket)—he felt a close fluttering in his ears and he became even more deliberate in his movements. He scattered the twigs and let the tension out of his neck. When he looked up, he saw that the larger cow had stepped toward him. Both animals stared at him with their flat dark eyes; they swayed dumbly. Angus kicked the stool over, and at the sound both cows started and averted their gaze.

At the house, his sister already had the fire going. He handed her the milk and she took it to the kitchen. When she sat back down, he could see her thoughts were elsewhere but that she was content. He did not wish to confront or unsettle her, not now. He did not need to know why she'd made them. What mattered was that he'd found them before their father had. He took the cloth from his pocket and laid it in the fire, but if his sister noticed she made no indication.

—I like the leaves this time of year, she finally said. It's like it happened overnight.

—I do too, Angus said.

The house was clean and ordered, as their father had directed. They were as prepared as they would be. Angus looked toward the window. Annabel sang quietly. The sun tracked slowly across the sky and they sat together for a long time without talking.

THEIR FATHER RETURNED as the day was dimming, later than anticipated. Angus had gone outside to pull the evening wood, and as he stood near the shed, he felt his gaze drawn down to the southern edge of their property. His father was a tall man. Though he'd thinned, he was still imposing in his black town clothes, head bent as he turned up the long dirt path to their house. Upon leaving, he'd told them only that he was traveling to Boston to seek counsel. Now, his hands swung freely, and though he wore the same clothes he'd left in four days ago, he no longer carried his satchel. Angus raised a hand in greeting, but though his father saw him, though Angus saw his head tilt and glimpsed, even from this distance, his drawn expression and sunken gray eyes, he did not break stride nor raise his hand in acknowledgment of his son.

He called to his sister and she came to the door. They

received him side by side, wordlessly, and parted as he drew near. At the threshold he stopped and looked down at his children. He did not smile, he did not endear himself, but Angus thought he saw some of the firmness leave his shoulders. From his outer pocket, he pulled two small, bound books and held them carefully.

—This is my greeting, he said. You are to put them under your pillow. And read them when you have time.

Angus asked if there was any news. His father gave no answer. They took the small books and their father entered the house. Near the fire he stopped.

—I feel as though I've been walking for days, he said. For a minute or two he warmed his hands. Then he announced his intention to rest and locked himself in his bedroom.

They had no dinner. Night descended, a heavy curtain, and their father did not emerge from his room. Angus sat with his sister near the fire. He watched her carefully for any start or sign. She sat perfectly still, gazing intently at the slow-burning wood. Since their mother had passed, their father demanded a rigor of them they could neither understand nor anticipate, and they had practiced their silence in his presence. Eventually, Angus opened the small book his father had handed him and read enough to ask his sister for hers. She gave it to him without complaint.

—I'm thinking of her now, Annabel finally said.

—You shouldn't, Angus said. He knew he should reach for her, but he did not.

—I just wanted to tell you, she said. She laced her fingers in front of her chest and brought them to her lap. I don't feel sick, she said. I'm just thinking of her.

Angus pressed his palms together. Soon he felt her presence in the room and could not push it away. Her illness had been a spiritual one, and this was their mother now: an impression, a flickering—a feeling to be hushed. When the doctor arrived, brought by their father, they'd watched him administer his thick fingers to her body as she cried out. They'd been told to wait outside. Later he'd questioned the children about what they'd seen, and Angus had looked into his strange face and answered honestly— he'd watched as she'd become anguished at the sight of animals or was otherwise touched by something he could not see. She spoke of dark figures, of a mist that came from the woods. Pain entered the room, passed through her, brought a heaviness to her bed. Their father was frightened, and from his sternness they took their cues. They stood by her side and winced at her touch as she called for them. My children, she'd said, then stopped speaking altogether. They could not deny the bruises on her body. *This is not uncommon*, the doctor had said. *One hopes it does not spread.* Their father, a strange light in his eyes, had said nothing as they removed her from the house. Two members of their church had come the next day to help their father dispose of her belongings. They'd looked both sorrowfully and fearfully at the children.

The next few months had been desperate, bleak, and silent at home. Their father, always stern, became remote and hard in his practice. In the house, he took to new habits: squaring the furniture in each room; scrubbing the mantle of soot upon waking. They felt his anger growing. He showed them neither attention nor kindness. His punishments became erratic and severe. He'd forbidden them to leave the property, and when he was home, he hovered over the two of them like a heavy sky that opened and flashed without warning. He took to retiring before dark so that he might wake in the deepest part of the night to read and pray. Angus had heard him from their bedroom, silently reading and writing, the turn of a heavy page, a sigh, a small plea. Occasionally a harsher sound had come under the door, a sharp and erratic whispering that kept both him and his sister pressed firmly to their beds, waiting only for morning, when the house, no longer of the night, returned to its recognizable shape.

Without being instructed, they knew not to ask of their mother and to bury their accusations. They missed and spoke of her only to each other. In dreams, they understood what they had done; but upon waking it was less clear what was required of them now. They had failed to go to her. Their father had brought the doctor, and then she was gone. She had never been happy, but she was theirs. Now their father was the only person they saw. He left the house during the night, and came back in the morning, bringing with him no news, only a torment that clung to his dark coat like dew frost.

Now, near the fire, with their father home, Angus tried to remember his mother's face and he saw only Annabel's.

—If you look closely, she said, in the embers you can imagine a small village. Lit up at night, during the winter.

—I see it, he said. There are people everywhere.

Eventually, the fire quieted and neither child reached for wood.

That night, Angus held his sister's hand and spoke

softly to her in bed until she fell asleep. No visions came. No disturbances, no kicks. He woke only once, hours later, to the sound of his father pacing the room outside their bedroom door, slow footsteps that whispered across the wide, cold boards and gathered themselves at the foot of his heart.

THE NEXT MORNING BROUGHT RAIN. Their father sat with them as they read, eyes closed, as still as a painting as they recited the chapters, passed the book, and recited again. Watching him, Angus wondered if he was sleeping, or was even there in the room with them at all. But when Annabel stuttered a phrase or asked a question, his eyes fluttered open and he issued a correction or a terse answer, his sternness returned. Angus had told him upon waking about the chickens, and about the foxes that must've taken them, and quietly, in the night, but he'd only nodded, calm, unsurprised. Was she frightened? he'd asked. And Angus had said they both had been, but not overly so.

After he put the book away, he sent them to the barn. When they returned with the milk, he stood in the door and instructed them to go to town for eggs, since they now had none of their own.

—We haven't been for months, Angus said.

—You'll remember the path, his father replied. Then, more softly, he said: You will be welcomed. I have done good work.

To be back by nightfall they would have to leave now. Angus retrieved his coat from the back of the kitchen door and brought his sister's as well. Their father said nothing upon their departure, but Angus felt his eyes on them as they made their way down the narrow path that led away from the house. At the veer, Angus quickly turned, and saw their father had disappeared inside and closed the door.

The path was narrow and cut through dense growth. In the summer, the light shone through and cast brilliant shadows, mottling the dirt underfoot, but now the yellowed leaves had begun to fall, and the gray sky, and the morning's rain: the path was black mud, and suckled their boots. When they could, they walked adjacent, letting small finger branches brush and whisk over their coats. They did not speak much. Annabel, walking ahead, picked a blade of tall grass and tucked it behind her ear.

—I've missed this, Annabel finally said.

—We shouldn't linger, Angus said. But he felt at ease too.

The trip usually took an hour, but it felt to Angus, upon breaking through their path to the main road that led to the village, as if much more time had passed. The sun was not visible in the sky and cast no shadow, but the wetness had returned, and it seemed as though a low fog was settling. He took Annabel's hand, a cold touch. A carriage approached and they stepped aside. They followed the road until they found themselves in the wide square that gave shape to the village. They made their way past the small buildings and houses. Angus wondered if they would see anyone they knew, but even as the few people they passed stopped to stare at them, he saw no one he recognized.

—They're looking, Annabel said.

—I know, he said, and instructed her to put her hood up. He did the same.

Windows were covered with cloth; storefronts stood empty. Very few people walked outside. A brown horse, tied up, unsaddled, jerked his head against a post. They found the store they were looking for and knocked. A young girl opened and let them in.

Inside, it was warm—a full fire cracked the air, drove the wet out—and Annabel cupped her hands near it as Angus collected the eggs. At the counter, he mentioned his father's name. The man quickly snapped the ledger closed.

—Take what you need, he said. He was looking intently and unkindly at Annabel, who, Angus could see, had heard and was working to keep her eyes on the fire. The girl who had let them in had disappeared.

—Thank you, Angus said. He bundled the eggs and tucked them under his arm. The man made no reply, but looked at Annabel as if she had stolen something.

—What's under your coat? the man said.

—We're leaving, Angus said, and Annabel followed him out.

—That man was afraid of us, Annabel said when they were back on the road.

—That's not true, Angus said. He pulled her close, but she shrugged him off.

—It is, she said.

—Don't think about it, Angus said.

They walked a different path through the village on the way home, one that took them past their old school and the church. A richness of swallows banked overhead, black dots; the sound of a hammer on steel sharpened their ears.

—They're just birds, Angus said when Annabel winced.

They crossed the green. As they rounded the corner near the church, they saw a crowd had gathered around a man who was speaking on an elevated platform. Angus recognized him immediately and tried to steer Annabel away, but she'd seen him too: it was the doctor who had come to the house with their father. It was impossible to hear what he was saying. He paced back and forth. He was not a tall man, but he wore a large billed hat and seemed bigger, somehow, than Angus remembered. Next to him on the platform stood a thin woman, dressed in black, who looked down at her feet. The doctor pointed at her, and she nodded, or shook her head. The crowd formed a thick, silent circle around the two of them but was quiet. Angus yanked at his sister's arm, but she shook him off.

—It's time for us to go, he said, and squeezed her hand.

—What's going to happen? she said.

—It's not our business, Angus said.

A call went up from the crowd. Finally, Annabel assented. As they turned to leave, a woman near the back of the circle slowly turned and looked at them. Her face, from that distance, looked to Angus not like a face at all, but an expressionless mask. She motioned toward them, but when they did not come, she turned her attention back to the doctor.

They retraced their steps until they found themselves back in the town square. They followed the road, found the seam in the woods that gave way to the dirt path that would take them home. Neither wanted to return so soon, but it would be dark, and there was nowhere else for them to go.

THEIR FATHER WAS NOT at the house when they arrived. They were used to it at this point, these night entrances and exits, and when they had the house to themselves, Angus couldn't help thinking this could be their life, just the two of them: unseen, left alone, out from under their father's moods. But their father always returned—sometimes exhausted, sometimes lit from within—and never told them where he'd been or why he'd left or what he'd seen. In the months following their mother's death, Angus had stayed up with him, near the fire; but whatever streamed darkly across his father's mind went unshared. Occasionally he'd felt his father's gaze on his back and it registered coldly; but when he turned, the gaze transformed, and Angus could no longer locate the ill will he was so certain of. One thing he was certain of, however: his father, a strong, tall man, had grown sinewy these last few months, his arms thinned and his hands veined, almost as if he were disappearing into himself, leaving the world for someplace even more stern and unforgiving. *We cannot call what we did a mistake*, he had said to Angus one night while Annabel was asleep. *It was she*, he said, *who did what she shouldn't have*. Angus had nodded and said nothing. He understood when his father was inviting him to speak and when his silence was required. *Where do you go at night?* Angus asked, but his father did not respond. *I've given you everything you need*, he finally said. *I've done my best.* With him they'd walked to the village to see their mother's body. With him they'd come home through the darkening woods in silence. Only later had Annabel shown Angus the poppets their mother had left for them—a boy and a girl, made from twisted sticks, eyes of dried berries. She had fit them under their bed, where the hard mattress met the frame.

That night they were alone, but pretended they were not. They remained alert until they could stay awake no longer. Annabel was still, but Angus dreamed. In this dream, a great rush of swallows dipped across a snow-covered pasture, which he knew, though he didn't recognize it, to be their property. And when he woke it was to his sister, gently comforting him, whispering in his ear. She was talking about their mother, and Angus let her. She was kind, his sister was saying. She was beautiful. She was ours.

WHEN THEY WOKE, the house was still and empty. In the quiet of the morning they passed the book to each other, finished, and their father had not returned. The wind came up, bringing with it a brief rain. After lunch the weather calmed, and the two of them walked the property, listening to the woods and the encroaching season. Annabel touched their mother's tree. The paths on the property crossed, converged, knit together only to split unexpectedly. Some Angus had cut with his father. Others were natural, the range of deer and bear, of other night animals.

—Where do you think he is? Annabel finally said.

—I don't know, Angus said.

He followed his sister, snapping twigs. He cleared the path of small rocks. The leaves were almost gone; the cold hastening. The pond—that was where they were going, where his sister said she wanted to go—was ringed by willows, and the dirt path turned to mud as they came closer. In the winter, the pond froze with a thin layer of shallow, glinting ice that sucked the shore, but it was too early for that, and as the two of them made their way carefully around the soft and giving grass, Angus was struck by the illusion of depth given by the water. They swam this pond in the summer, careful to keep their feet from the grabbing mud—he knew the water to be shallow save for the very center. But now, standing on the northern bank, he was taken by the feeling that the pond had grown both wide and deep since he'd last swum across. He picked a small rock from under his boot and tossed it. The water accepted the stone and sent a small wave circling back to him.

—Don't do that, his sister said. Please.

—Why not? he said, but she didn't answer. He looked across the water at the trees and then looked back to her. She stood a few feet away. Though she was bundled against the cold, Angus could see she was shivering. Her long hair hid mostly under a cap, but a few strands, picked up by the wind, played in front of her face and caught in the corner of her mouth. This had been their favorite spot. Their father, who could not swim, never joined them here.

—Angus, his sister said, and showed him. In her hands she held two poppets like the ones their mother had left them.

—Why are you making those? Angus said.

She said nothing. Angus watched closely.

—Stop. You know what will happen.

—I'm not making them. I found them. They were in my coat. She began to squeeze the figures, then seemed frightened by what she was doing.

—Don't lie, Angus said. Stop.

He reached for the figures, but she thrust them back into her pockets. He grabbed her coat at the shoulders. At his touch, her knees gave, and he struggled to keep her standing, off the grass, away from the mud. She began to fight but he held her still. He felt a great sadness well, and then a panic. He thought he might be on the verge of violence. He shook her twice until she grabbed at him, and then they were both sitting on the wet bank.

—You can't have them, she said. She was crying.

—Give them to me. Give them to me and we'll bury them.

—It's getting worse.

Angus looked to the pond. The wind picked up and he watched a leaf fall from one of the tall trees, slowly twist, and land on the surface of the water.

—Stop, he said again. He was crying now.

—It's her, Annabel said. Angus knew she was talking about their mother. She can hear us, Annabel said.

—Give them to me, he said, reaching now for her pockets. Eventually she heard him and drew the figures from her coat. He felt no charge at their touch, they had no weight. He unwound them, stood, and found a rock. With the twine he wrapped what he could around the rock, threw the rock far into the water, and then his sister lay back in the grass.

He waited as she kicked, and then, as the gasping began, he went to hold her. She batted the air in front of her face with her hands, but Angus saw nothing. Eventually, he lifted her from the grass, and they made their way back to the house. He put her in bed, washed her clothes. His fear was a live thing; then, as the fire he started took hold of the room, that fear unbraided and thinned into strands and he found he could control it. He made dinner, and Annabel ate. Eventually, their father came home. They greeted him quietly and tried not to shrink as he took himself to bed.

Later that night, when he heard his father outside their door, pacing then settling, feeding the fire, Angus left his sleeping sister and walked quietly to the foot of their bed. Through his window, he could see the dark night, and the small glow pressing from the window of the main room where his father sat. It threw a circumscribed circle of light on the path that led away from the house. Beyond that was the woods, then the village, and then what he did not know. His panic returned and he pushed it down. When it seemed his father had settled, he made his way to their bedroom door, opened it, and slipped out. His father was fully dressed. Open before him was a book he was not reading.

—She might have gotten better, Angus said.

—Don't speak, his father said. It would not have happened. It has happened nowhere else.

—We might have done differently.

His father coughed and reached with his hand to cover his mouth.

—A man should not have children, he finally said. It

was your mother who left us. It was she who answered what she should not have. I tried and she did not listen. You are wrong. About everything you are wrong. He coughed again. Have you noticed the swallows? he said. They've returned.

Angus said he had not.

—You must remember to always tell the truth.

—I have seen no swallows, Angus said, and closed his eyes.

His father lay the iron down near the hearth and turned so his back was to his son. The conversation was over. Eventually Angus took himself back to bed. His sister shifted and released the blankets, reached for his hand.

Sometime later he heard his father stand, and then he heard the latch of the front door, a small metallic click, and the quick swing of the hinges. And then the house settled into a complete, recursive silence.

MORNING CAME, and with it the work of the day. Their father cut in the backfield while Angus and his sister gathered and tied the grass. It was slow work. The day was cold. Angus watched his sister closely—their father was far enough away that he might be able to help her before anything caught his attention—but Annabel showed no sign of trouble. She was not happy, but she hummed as she worked, tying bunches, scuffing her boots after bugs while Angus did the lifting. Angus guessed she was as wary as he was, as vigilant, but he could not know. She seemed exhausted. Their father, sweat-drenched, swung the scythe in a stiff-backed, rhythmic way. Only once did Annabel startle, and stare deeply across the field to the woods. Angus followed her eyes but could see nothing himself, and Annabel, aware of the slip, bent herself more fully to the work. Their father, consumed by the balanced shushing of his blade, saw none of this.

They finished and as the sun began its descent, they followed their father inside. Once in the kitchen, their father sat rigidly at the table in the corner as the children prepared the food.

—Almost winter, he said.

—Yes, Angus said. He dipped three cups and set the milk on the table. Annabel reached for a small bowl to prepare the eggs. He searched for something else to say but could think of nothing. As he brought the milk to his mouth, he smelled foulness.

—It's soured, he said. He quickly put his cup down. Don't drink it.

—It's from this morning, his father said.

It was then that it happened. Annabel cried out and Angus turned at the sound. She now stood with her hand pressed tightly against her mouth in an attempt to reclaim the noise. It was too late. Her knees buckled, recovered, and she walked quickly across the kitchen. *Move*, he thought. He stood and crossed to where she'd been standing. She was now near the door and looked at him pleadingly. With her hands she began smoothing the front of her dress. Then he looked in the bowl where she had cracked the eggs. Curled at the bottom of the bowl were two half-formed chicks, red and dark, spread with sparse black feathers. They were beaked but had no legs.

—What is it? his father said.

—Nothing, Angus said. He tried to cover the bowl but was too slow and his father stood beside him.

—What is it? he said.

—Nothing, Angus said.

His father put a hand on his shoulder and pushed him out of the way. Angus could not read his expression.

—Who has touched these? he said. Shaking, he reached for the remaining eggs and slowly cracked each into the bowl. Look! he said, and brought the bowl to Angus. His hands were white from the grip. In the pool of glassy albumen Angus counted four more malformations.

—Who has touched these eggs? he said again. He spoke quietly now and was looking only at Annabel. She did not return his gaze.

—We all have, Angus said.

—I have not, he said. Carefully, he set the bowl by the kitchen door. When he stood, his eyes were bright.

—Undress, he said to Annabel.

—I touched them, Angus said.

—Undress, he said again, this time to both of his children. I'm not going to ask again.

Angus could feel his sister, next to him, struggling to stay on her feet. He could not look at her. He slowly took off his shirt. He loosened his pants and let them fall. Finally, he glanced at Annabel and saw she had done the same, her dress now on the floor, her eyes downcast. With shame he saw the marks he'd left on her arms when he'd grabbed her near the pond. But they were far from the only marks on her, and Angus saw his father tremble at the sight of his daughter's bruised body.

—She fell from a tree, Angus said. You were gone.

—Do not lie, he said.

—She's fine, Angus said.

—Do not lie, he said again. He instructed them to kneel and when they did, he turned and walked from the kitchen. Annabel began to cry. She tried to speak but no sound left her throat. Angus felt his mind go empty. His father was too big. There would be nothing he could do. I'm sorry, he told his sister. She did not move. If she heard him, she made no indication. When their father returned, he wore a new expression. He was no longer afraid or surprised. He appeared remote and focused, and to Angus almost unrecognizable, as though this was a man they didn't know, someone else wearing their father's face. But that impression was fleeting. In one hand he held a rag, and in the other he held a switch.

He'd beaten them before, but not like this. He swung for the backs of their arms and feet, his breathing deep and rhythmic and unhurried.

When the punishment finally stopped, their father broke the switch and stepped outside. It had grown dark. Angus reached for his sister's hand. She did not take it. When their father finally returned, he carried a stouter branch. He was sweating. Neither child moved.

—Someone is calling for you, he finally said. I will show him out. He stood before them and raised the thick switch and cut the air once, twice, across the heavy distance between them, then walked toward Angus and roughly pressed the switch to his son's chest.

—You are a fearful boy, he said. He was swaying, slightly, and looked toward the open back door. I am asking for your help.

—She has a fever, Angus said. She caught a chill.

Their father's expression did not change.

—Neither of you is to leave this house, he finally said.

Angus nodded. His legs radiated sharp pain. Annabel had gathered her clothes and was holding them tightly.

—Take her to bed, and see to her, he said. Do your best. He reached for the bowl and carefully tucked it under his arm. He left the kitchen and walked out of the house.

—It's going to be all right, Angus said. It's going to be all right. He reached for Annabel's elbow, and, careful not to touch the welts blossoming on her arms, helped her to her feet.

—Annabel, he said, and took her to their room. Whatever had been happening—it was now coming to a close. The children could feel that. That night, Annabel talked and Angus made no effort to shush her. She spoke of a red sky, and of a golden thread wrapped around her hair. He'd tended carefully to the welts on her legs and arms, and she had not winced as he cleaned and dressed her. He waited for her to kick and yell, but she did not. Then she'd cleaned his wounds and helped him into his shirt. There is a world outside of this one, she said as they lay down. Angus asked her to describe it, and she did.

The night came through their window and bathed them in darkness. It seemed, perhaps, that this night would not end. It was a welcome thought.

Later, when Annabel stiffened, he held her gently in his arms. He put a corner of their blanket in her mouth to stifle her cries. He could not look at her eyes as they rolled back, but when she quieted, he put his hand to her brow and dabbed at the small amount of blood that had run from her nose. Then she finally slept, and Angus felt her isolation completely.

THE DOCTOR ARRIVED two days later. It seemed as though the house had summoned him itself. Angus saw him from afar: he'd been moving grass to the barn, and when he turned up the path to the house the doctor appeared near the mouth of the woods as though he were the breath of breeze himself. He carried a small case and was dressed in an oversized brown coat. He wore the same wide-brimmed hat they'd seen covering his head, shading his round and drooping face, in the village. The wind picked up. On the ground near where the doctor stood was a larger case, and behind that case stood their father.

Angus walked quickly to the house and called for his sister but received no answer. He left the milk in the kitchen and tried to calm himself. When he went to their bedroom, he saw Annabel sitting rigidly on their bed.

—He's here, she said.

—I know, Angus said. In her hands she held one of the poppets their mother had made. Come on, he said. He took the figure from her and returned it to its hiding place. He didn't have time to take it apart. Come on.

She was pale, her hair tucked roughly behind her ears.

—Are you prepared?

—Yes, she said.

She stood. Angus unrolled his sleeves and then rolled them again. They heard the front door open and there was nothing to do but stand and go to their father.

When they entered the room, the doctor turned from where he'd been warming himself against the fire. He was a small man. Something about his appearance was off: his arms were too long for his body, or his legs too short. His hat, which he had not removed, no longer cast a shadow over his face. His hands were gloved. With a small flourish, he took off his hat and placed it on their father's chair. His black hair was unkempt, a nest.

—These woods, he said, are thicker than I remember.

—We've fallen down with our cutting, their father said.

The doctor nodded. He asked for water and their father returned with a cup. He drank in one long pull and set the cup on the table. He spoke nothing of the village, or of his reason for visiting, but he didn't need to. Angus knew his father, whose eyes were alert, had sent for him and brought him here.

—I've had little rest, the doctor finally said. He sighed. I remember this house. This living room. Your mother, he said, turning to Angus. She lay right here. He gestured carefully with both gloved hands, articulating the area where they'd placed the small mattress on the floor, the sweat-soaked pillow. And you, above her.

—We've done as you suggested, their father said. This home is bare and scrubbed.

The doctor looked at Annabel, then back to the fire.

—Three separate farms in the last month, he said. No crops grow. In the village it is no better. Children refuse to eat.

—Until two days ago, I had seen nothing, their father said. And I have been watchful.

—And strict?

—We read every day, their father replied.

—No more could be asked, the doctor said. He walked the room slowly, examining windows, running his finger along the frame. Angus watched as Annabel began to shift her weight back and forth. Her eyes remained on the fire.

—I will ask for some privacy with the children, the doctor finally said.

Angus saw his father's expression turn. His eyes darkened. He made no move to leave.

— If you don't mind, the doctor said.

—No, their father finally said. He left and shut the door behind him.

The doctor turned to the fire. Finally, he asked if they'd seen the swallows, and when Angus answered no, he turned and smiled. That's right, he said. There are no swallows. His teeth were crowded atop one another. He picked his hat from the stool and handed it to Angus.

—Please, he said, sit.

Angus did as he was told. Annabel remained standing.

—Your father, he began, has traveled a great distance, and is still traveling. But he is concerned. And he loves you very much. You are dear to him.

Neither Angus nor his sister lifted their eyes from the floor.

—This is delicate, the doctor finally said. I will speak to your sister first, and then I will call for you.

Angus remembered no delicacy from this man, but he could think of nothing to do for his sister that would not bring more suspicion. When their mother had been examined, Angus had paced the entryway until the doctor demanded he stop. His sister had cried out and had to be held by their father. They'd made things worse by becoming upset.

Now the doctor sighed and, carrying his small case, moved with Annabel into their bedroom and shut the door.

He heard no sound from their room, no thrashing, no cries. Stillness was required in the presence of this man. The fire cracked, splintered, burned itself, glowing, down to embers. At first Angus had been afraid to move, and now, with the doctor's heavy hat on his lap, he found he no longer wished to move at all. He was aware of time passing. The silence in the house deepened. He tried to imagine his sister and he called to her in his head, but then his mind settled and emptied. At some point, he sensed he was no longer alone in the room and he saw his father's pale face at the window, pressed to the glass. He eyes were like burning pieces of coal. His mouth hung open. He looked to Angus like anger itself, and he was afraid; but soon his father's features blended with the darkness and his face became a blank mask: an image of his father, but not he. Angus looked away. When he looked again, his father had disappeared.

Finally, the door opened and the doctor stood in front of him.

—She needs rest, he said, and closed the bedroom door. He walked to Angus and set his small case on the floor. Does that door have a lock? he asked, and Angus shook his head. No matter, he said. He instructed Angus to stoke the fire, and Angus stood as if suddenly released.

—What have you seen, the doctor said when Angus sat back down.

—Nothing, Angus said.

Now the doctor moved very close and stretched his gloved hands in front of him. He began using his thick fingers on Angus's arm. It's all right, he said. Angus said nothing. Roll up your sleeve, he said. Angus did, and when the doctor touched him again, he felt the air leave his body. Your sister is in an unusual state, the doctor said. And I need your help. He took a small glass vial from his case and held it to Angus's forearm. Angus felt a pressure, as though the glass were a small mouth sucking at his skin.

—Has she been calling out? the doctor said.

Angus shook his head.

—I don't believe you, the doctor said. Angus began to feel a small circle of heat form on his arm where the vial touched his skin. You can tell me, the doctor said.

—She is in pain, Angus said.

—I know.

Angus's vision blurred. He wiped at his eyes with his free hand and was suddenly cold.

—My father's watching, he said.

The doctor stiffened. He looked up from his small case and clasped his hands together, thick fingers knitted in front of his chest. The vial that held on Angus's arm did not release. He felt his throat go warm.

—He's everywhere.

—Then tell it to me in my ear, the doctor said and leaned close.

It seemed to Angus that the two of them were no longer talking to each other. Or, they were talking, but without sound. The small doctor tilted his head so that his eyes fixed on the floor and Angus leaned forward so there was no distance between them.

—You poor child, the doctor finally said. He reached out and put a gloved hand over Angus's ear, then dropped it. He packed his case. And when he stood to leave, Angus saw his sister in the doorway to their room, hidden behind the half-shut door.

THEY HAD NO DINNER. When their father returned to the house, he pulled the book from the shelf and they read together. He asked them no questions about the visit, and as the night went on and true darkness took hold of the woods outside, Angus found himself wondering if the doctor had been there at all. Nothing in the house had changed. There had been no yelling, no crying like last time. But when he saw the red circle on his forearm he knew. When he looked at his sister and saw she had withdrawn, completely, into herself, he knew. The doctor had come and had pulled them both to him, as he had before.

Finally, their father closed the book. He stood and embraced his children. When he held Angus, it felt to Angus as though he were leaning into the trunk of a large tree. With Annabel, he was more tentative, but he enveloped her nonetheless and held her tightly.

—Tomorrow will come, he finally said, and sent them away.

ANGUS KNEW THAT neither he nor his sister would sleep, but for a long time they did not speak. They waited in their room until their father stopped his pacing, until the light from the fire dimmed under the door, and they were sure he had taken himself to bed.

—She's here, Annabel finally said. She was with me.

Angus said nothing.

—And she forgives us.

—What did you tell him? Angus said.

—I don't remember, she said. It felt like I wasn't even there. Then she said, Are you afraid?

—I am, Angus said.

—Don't be, she told him. I'm not.

The wind tore briefly at the shingles of the house, then relented. The night spun out and wove itself around the two of them.

AND WHEN THEY DID COME, Angus saw them from the small window in their room. Ten to twelve lanterns swung up the path, a slow and deliberate constellation that lit the woods. He called his sister. He heard the latch on the front door and knew their father had left them.

He went to their bed, made it, and returned to the window.

—Annabel, he said.

—No, she said.

—Annabel, he said.

—It's what I wanted, she said.

The lanterns were closer now, and gave shape to the night outside. Someone was singing, a low sound that cut through the house and pressed across the field. She held out her hand, and Angus took it. Her hand was warm, and in his he sensed a deep heat blooming. The moon shone through the branches of the elm in their yard. When they were younger, Annabel had always been the first to laugh, his mother's favorite. Images came to him, some he couldn't place. The dark path through the woods; frost on the leaves; a robin drying its wings. His mother, in light, applying pressure to his fevered head. The heat from his sister's touch moved up his arm and spread across his shoulders. He had her hand and she would not let go. Behind him came a sound like water rushing over rocks. He stood in the room, but it was no longer theirs. You know what's coming next, his mother said. But Angus didn't know. Annabel, he said, but she wouldn't answer. It was easier this way, and it was like nothing he'd felt before.

FARTHEST SOUTH
\\\\\\\\

EACH DAY HE WAKES to cold light, dark waves, and a
shifting horizon line, the flap of canvas sails, the creak
of a keeling ship. There has been nothing else for weeks.
He's ill and cannot get comfortable. His eyes are deep blue,
piercing, red-rimmed, expressively empty, and they've refused to adjust to the gloom of his cabin. Below deck there
is only darkness, but topside, he knows, there is limitless white light. He hauls himself up the aft companion-
way and from the deck looks at the ice shelf ahead of him.
It rises from the ocean like a set of giant's teeth. *You are
where you are*, he thinks, and his heart leaps, settles, flattens out.

"GOOD MORNING." AT HIS SIDE stands an emperor penguin, cheerful companion, loyal friend. My grandfather has named him Franklin, after one of his favorite dogs from home. When he waddles across the deck, he reminds my grandfather of a black and white channel buoy that bobbed near his home cove when he was a child. "Shall I tell the children we've arrived?" Franklin asks.

"Not yet," says my grandfather. A thought forms in his skull and evaporates. The ship dips with the swell, and he steadies himself against the roll. His mind is shorting out. He thinks: *the sea is like . . . is like . . . is like . . . the sea.*

A bolt of freezing sea wind bores an acid tunnel to the back of his throat. He coughs into a handkerchief. Blood.

"On second thought," he says, "yes."

Once his companion leaves, he folds the handkerchief twice, remembers it was a gift from his own children, from his wife, and throws it overside. No need to worry anyone. The stained piece of cloth flutters and dips on the wind like an enormous white butterfly before settling atop the leaden water, saturating, and sinking. *Onward*, he thinks.

THE CHILDREN APPEAR ON DECK. There are twenty-five of them, little blond Norsemen. They've read my grandfather's books; they are excited to be a part of this expedition. Below deck, they've made dolls out of sticks and sailcloth, pulled clothes from the communal chest, staged elaborate plays. They've helped with dinner and cleaned their plates; they'll do whatever Franklin asks of them. They've shown no greenness on the waves. Looking at them now, however, my grandfather realizes he cannot tell them apart. The only name he can remember is Hjalmar. But which one is Hjalmar? He was one of the smaller boys. Not here, now. Or is he?

"THAT," MY GRANDFATHER SAYS, and gestures over the bow toward the ice shelf, "is McMurdo Bay. If you follow my finger's line, you will see Mount Erebus and Mount Terror. They are ice volcanoes, named for ships."

The children cheer, punch their fists, and look excitedly in the direction he is pointing. If all goes well, their expedition will go like this: depot, depot, depot, rookery, depot, pole. They will cross the barrier ice with Victoria Land rising to the west; they will climb the pressure ridge abutting the Queen Maud Mountains, traverse the white and brown glacier, and return under the watchful eye of Mount Helmer Hanssen. The weather will be bleak and howling, the journey miserable, but the sled dogs will help them, and the reward will be great. They will write their own books. Some of the children, he notices, are hugging one another.

My grandfather sweeps his hands wide, then returns them to the deep pockets of his heavy woolen coat. He gazes at his young crew and works to bury the expression he feels forming. The children peek out at him from their drawn hoods. *They are a blessing, not a burden*, he thinks. He coughs once, twice. It's productive. He spits. "Our journey begins," he says, and Franklin pats his hand.

THEIR SHIP IS A THREE-MASTED, four-hundred-ton schooner, outfitted with a retractable rudder and propeller, a windmill for energy production, and a small camp stove in the galley. Her hull is wrapped in greenheart wood and she draws power from a triple-expansion steam engine. She is his own design, commissioned and built over two years in Larvik, a ship of astonishing beauty. He will be sad to leave her.

As they move farther into the floes, the Ross Ice Shelf forms a basin and all ocean sound drops away. There are no birds. They see neither walrus nor seal. The only noise comes from their small engine, lunging along. It feels to my grandfather like they are gliding into the frozen mouth of the world.

ONCE ANCHORED, THEY SPEND the day moving supplies from ship to ice, harnessing sled dogs, tuning sledge runners. In the evening, everyone gathers in the ship's main cabin for supper. It will be the last comfortable meal, my grandfather knows, and he's pleased to see everyone in such good spirits on the eve of their departure. Once the feast is over, the children tidy up, and Franklin lowers the lamp to begin one of his lessons. The children, in their shared sleeping bags, strain to listen. "Do not think of the cold," he says. "Instead, think of a moment that has brought you great happiness, and let that be the lantern that warms you. And as we progress, I'd like to remind you that penguins are the link between reptiles and the mainland birds you are familiar with. Evolutionary-wise, that is."

Outside it is −27 degrees Celsius, but inside, in the close and cramped ship's cabin, it's as warm as a bakery oven.

"Goodnight, young explorers," Franklin says, and extinguishes the lamp.

DARK NIGHT. LONG NIGHT. MY grandfather tightens the mouth of his sleeping bag. The wind picks up and rasps at the ship's rigging, asking to be let in. Not good. Not good. The pain in his ribs has returned, his tongue feels wooly. *Maybe*, my grandfather thinks, *they won't show up this time.* But his mind is a dark engine, and show up they do: a parade of floating heads, coming down the ship's corridor, bobbing toward him like paper lanterns on a string. Some wear balaclavas, some are hatless, some scurvied and bleeding from exposure and sour gums. Their dark eyes are filled with accusatory wonder. They do not blink. My grandfather nervously greets each frozen face as it floats around his cabin, some familiar, some not. Finally, the heads collect themselves in a pile near the foot of his bed.

"What do you *want*?" my grandfather says. The heads whisper quietly to one another—they seem amused by his predicament—and they do not answer.

Franklin, sleeping next to him, has not stirred. Finally, the heads begin to quiet down. They close their eyes for the night, they shut their incomprehensible mouths. They roll one by one out of the door and down the hallway and allow my grandfather to drift into his own heavying limbs and journey as he wishes to the small clapboard home of his youth, in Svalbard, and then to blacker sleep.

IN THE MORNING, he takes stock. Twenty-five children, twenty-two dogs, Franklin the penguin, and himself. Five sledges, each weighing two hundred and thirty-seven pounds. The dogs will take two, the children two, he and Franklin one. In a fur-lined pouch affixed to his hip, he has tucked the medical supplies, his sextant, a chronometer, his journal and pencils, and a roughly folded map detailing their projected route, known elevations, unexpected crevasses.

It is −32 degrees, with no wind from the south. It will only get colder as they trek across the barrier ice.

The children stand ready in their hats and harnesses. They are looking to my grandfather for some words of inspiration, encouragement, or perhaps even love, but his mind has gone elsewhere, it's a blank shimmering thing. Franklin clears his throat and gruffs with his beak at his preened feathers. The dogs are restless and yip to one another. Finally, my grandfather turns and says, "The difficult is what takes a little time; the impossible is what takes a little longer."

The children look perplexed.

Franklin sighs, gathers himself, secures his towline over his shoulder. "Gid-up," he says to the children, and they throw their hats in the air.

Across the ice they are pulling pemmican, sugar, butter, tents, plank wood for an igloo door, hoosh, rudimentary first-aid kits, amputation instruments, limes, lamps, socks, brandy, whisky, rum, matches.

In my grandfather's fur pouch is a photograph of Fridtjof Nansen and Frederick Jackson shaking hands at Franz Josef Land. It is the very moment they knew their winter on that infernal frozen island was over.

"Frederick Jackson," says my grandfather. Low light bounds off the ice directly in front of him. "Heavenly days."

THE FIRST WEEK IS SLOW GOING. Towlines get tangled, and, as they plod farther across the barrier ice, the snow becomes deeper, heavier; each step is met with an audible granular give. Each step is a sinking. Each step is like a rasping cough. The sun is a gel smear, dim on the horizon. The ice, in constant adjustment, cracks and groans; the sound is like tree limbs bending, breaking in heavy wind. Mount Erebus looms to the west, gently sloped, and in front of them they see the pressure ridge, jagged, licked and shaped by polar weather.

"Enchantment, wonder," says Franklin happily, pulling next to my grandfather. "Uncharted, limitless white."

"And," my grandfather says, "no more floating visitors, thank God."

"Hmmm?" Franklin says, but my grandfather is adjusting his harness, it's been biting his shoulder all morning, and doesn't reply.

Two miles a day over the ice, then break, then pen the dogs, then set up camp. Then eat, sleep, wake, roll up the tents, pack everything into the sledges, count the dogs, count the children, sight the route, mark the journal, pray for holding weather, head down, walk.

The children set up soccer pitches when they can, and under the low, gray sky kick around a ball made of frozen socks.

At night, my grandfather feeds the dogs Norse fish from tins, heats food for the children; he tells them stories of brave men and heroic sled dogs on the ice; and then, as they settle in—as the Primus stove is extinguished, and the light goes soft—Franklin stands to his full height and opens his black beak to the top of the tent to sing gently to the tired group. Some of the children join in with their sweet voices, a boys' choir falsetto, delicate and true if a little quavery. But most only mouth words until the melody lulls them to sleep, where in dream each is visited by his favorite dog from the pack.

"I didn't know you could sing like that," my grandfather whispers.

"You never asked," says Franklin shyly.

Later, in their tent, my grandfather admits he's worried about the pace they've established, the resilience of the children, the supplies they are towing, the increasing wind, the plunging cold, the dimming sun, and the fact that he still can't tell one child from another.

"Worry does not empty tomorrow of its sorrow," Franklin says and pats his hand. "It only empties today of its strength."

ONWARD THEY WALK, carving a straight line across the ineffable ice. Hours, days. They haul sledges up snowdrifts and skid down furrows, traverse glass ice and black ice, trek through a low red fog that hounds them for miles. They circumvent pressure ridges, narrowly escape sliding into a crevasse. They brace themselves against the cold and the wind, admire the view, stomp their feet to encourage circulation.

Expeditions have good days and bad days. These days have been good. *This continent is a blank canvas*, thinks my grandfather, *and we are its slow painters*.

At rest, Franklin conducts blister inspections on the children, oohing and aaahing; he asks them to be brave for his lancing, and rewards each with a small lump of sugar. They are trying to be resilient; they are doing their best. But before bed, when my grandfather reads aloud from his own book, Franklin sees exhaustion and boredom and frustration on their small faces, and now and then glimpses genuine fear.

"Exploration," my grandfather says warmly as he shuts the book, "is the *crucible* of the human imagination."

"And into notational night we go," Franklin says, lowering the lamps. "Good night, little seals."

The children answer, a quiet chorus, and Franklin and my grandfather bow through the flaps of their tent. The dogs sleep. There is no wind, no snow, and the sky is like an artist's rendition of sky, alive with brushed light. *This will not last*, my grandfather thinks.

"We never expected it to," Franklin says.

THAT NIGHT, THOUGH my grandfather's sleep has become less troubled, the heads do find him. They bob above the barrier ice like glowing, floating apples, each face deprived of oxygen, each cheek sunk. They file in, deep blue with black eyes, circle his bed, gather themselves in the corner of his tent. He pulls his sleeping bag over his head. In the darkness, he wills himself to feel gratitude; that is what they are here for. He tries to push this feeling into the room, wishes to say *there is nothing here but love,* but that is not what he feels. What he feels is terror, and he cannot speak. "Do you know where you are?" one of them asks. He will not answer.

When he wakes from these corridors he is shaking and shivering, covered in sweat, and there is no one for him to recognize, for the room is dark and empty. He listens for a sound that will tell him where he is. He hears the squeak of hospital shoes and whispered voices, some distant laughter.

He closes his eyes, opens them again. Franklin sleeps next to him now, he can see him in the dark, standing with his beak tucked low on his chest, his eyes firmly shut and dreaming, no doubt, of small fish darting through the flashing deep.

THE WEATHER TURNS, and the cold gets worse, the climb harder, the daily drudgery of an expedition such as this more numbing and rote. They make three nautical miles a day, but the parties move at a different pace, and the children are sluggish. As they close in on the pressure ridge that abuts the St. Edwards Range, my grandfather grows worried, for even from ten miles out he can see that it will be a climb like no other.

The less said about the weather, he writes that night in his journal, *the better.* The fog has cleared, but the cold has gripped. His breath frosts the paper, the pencil will not bite. He thaws the page with a close-held match he has trouble lighting.

The children have started to understand how this expedition will go. They take to hiding in their sleeping bags in the morning, they drag their feet. All but one has begun to complain about the food. All but one is slow to roll his gear and secure it on the sledge. And this one boy, my grandfather is pleased to see, is Hjalmar.

Hjalmar is not much of a puller. He is wanly complected, with pallid cheeks, delicate eyes. The other children don't like him. But he has shown a keen interest in navigation, and an exuberance for sighting that my grandfather feels should be encouraged. "Come, Hjalmar," he says, when they've stopped to repair one of the sled runners. He hands Hjalmar the navigation pouch, and the two of them trudge in snowshoes a quarter mile away from the group. "We are ten thousand feet above sea level," my grandfather says as they walk. He knows it's important to be impartial, and not to give preferential treatment to anyone in the traveling party, but he's become fond of this boy, and worries what will happen to him if left too much alone. At the camp, Franklin hammers away, tireless and cheerful, realigning and repairing the sledge while the other children stand around, expressing boredom.

"Those are the Queen Maud Mountains," my grandfather says, and points. "And beyond that, you'll find the King Edward Plateau."

It is while he is sighting the horizon with Hjalmar that a

cry goes up from the camp. Franklin is signaling to them, and, once he has their attention, points frantically. The children have spotted something due south. When my grandfather looks through his binoculars, he sees what seems to be a cairn of some kind. It's nestled within a gentle slope of snow that makes it nearly invisible against the ice.

"Not good," Franklin says, when my grandfather returns. He's nervously flicking his toes against ice.

"They've seen it," my grandfather says. "We have no choice."

THE CHILDREN WORK IN PAIRS to shovel through the drift, and soon they have cleared a path to what seems to be a tent from long ago. My grandfather chips the ice from the tent's frozen flaps, inhales deeply, then peels them wide for all to see.

The children gasp. It's as though he's drawn the curtain on a diorama in a natural science museum. Three men in fur hats sit frozen around an ancient stove facing one another. Their emaciated faces are deep brown, their eyes closed and sunk in the sockets. An open journal rests in one of their laps. The scene is oddly tranquil—they look comfortable, at peace. There is no smell. But it is impossible not to see the heap of bones stacked on one of their cots.

Franklin coughs and begins ushering the children out of the tent. "Those are chicken bones," he says, laughing nervously. "Imagine having chickens all the way out here!"

The children are perplexed. "Who are these shriveled people?" one of them asks. "Brave explorers," my grandfather intones. "Friends of mine." Carefully, he steps across the tent and pulls the journal from the lap of one of the frozen men. After he has read to his satisfaction, he turns to address his own party. "They did not find the pole," he says. "This," he gestures to the tent, "is as far as they got. They ran out of food. They grew weak. They gave up." The children say nothing. They look at one another and shuffle their feet. "This is *good* news," he says.

They close up the ancient tent and leave it to the weather. The sledge is repaired, the dogs are eager to move, and Franklin has gone silent. On the horizon, a mountain range stretches, brown and iceless, across their path. They should see the rookery as soon as they reach King Edward Plateau. Half a mile behind, the children hum and kick ice clods as they trundle along.

Friends, my grandfather is thinking. *Friends*. Now, as they walk, he finds himself lost in a strange sort of reverie. Each foothold is like a mark across his brain; his veins run warm; it feels as though he's weightless. A new pain begins at the base of his skull and braids around his chest. The ice pulls away from his feet; there's a plunge, and it's as though he's sliding down a chute into one of the earth's dark, endless fissures. There he sees his children, small, pulling for air, then growing; they are sullen, indifferent to him; he sees them with children of their own, images that flash by like a deck of shuffled cards. He takes another step, and then another. He sees his wife, Eva, and calls for her. The cold has crisped his throat; no sound.

He'd said nothing to her of his plans before he'd left. Her complaint was always that he preferred the ice to her, and though it's not true, he could never correct her in a way that settled the issue.

She is a face carved into the brown range in front of them, now. She is in the low clouds. She is leaning over him, touching his cheek; she is old, he is the cause of her sorrow; she is small in this impersonal room of theirs; she turns from him, crosses the bright, tiled floor; she closes the curtains and then she is gone. He has always been the cause of her sorrow. He regrets that now.

EXCELLENT DAY, BEAUTIFUL DAY. They make eight nautical miles and camp themselves on the other side of the range. The mountains are imposing, but my grandfather suspects that they will have less trouble once they pull over the ice ridges that smooth into the plateau than they have had on the journey so far. They are steep mountains, glacially cut, and they are pleasantly disorienting to see up close. All of the children know how to ski and, after setting up camp, take to the slopes with abandon. Franklin delights everyone by waddling halfway up a gentle slope, whooping like a crane, and turning to luge down on his belly.

That night in the tent, the children put on a play. They've dressed the dogs as seals and use an overturned sledge as their ship. Everyone laughs, and there is a heroic swell, a moment of doubt, a great drift, and then finally vindication, a safe transport home, a hero's parade. My grandfather is deeply touched. In the third act, Hjalmar stands suddenly, and begins a rendition of *Ja, vi el-*

sker dette landet. His fragile voice pushes beyond the tent and out on to the ice, through the sifting fog, back to their ship. The other children have forgotten their lines, but join him in the refrain: *Yes, we love this country / As it rises forth / Love it and think of our father and mother / And the saga-night that lays / Dreams upon our earth.*

When he's finished, there is a deep and long quiet.

"I've never heard that before," Franklin says. "Bravo."

"Hjalmar," says my grandfather. "You have an astonishing voice. And a long, distinguished career on the stage ahead of you."

Hjalmar nods, a blush beginning at his ears. All the other children stand and bow. A reading that afternoon placed them at 87° 40' S. The play is complete.

IN THE MORNING, they trudge and trundle over rock and ice, sledges clattering, sending up shouts of alarm. Finally, the range flattens and the party quiets down, but still threat and danger lurk everywhere, and this leg . . . feels different. Crevasses open up in front of them and drop three hundred feet into glacial caves. Nesting terns call sharply from the bare mountain walls. "Is that a warning?" the children ask. "An omen?"

"No," Franklin replies. "Those are just stupid birds."

They come out the other side, but it's taken three days and they are not intact: blisters have become infected, lethargy is sinking in, there are rumblings of wanting to return home. The children's goggles fog, their hats are too tight. Their gloves, once wet, won't dry. *Stop complaining,* my grandfather wants to shout, but he knows that will get him nowhere.

They set up camp on the southern edge of the range and pen the dogs. As the food heats up, Franklin pulls my grandfather aside and asks him to acknowledge what they both know is approaching but have not mentioned: that every day the sun sinks lower and lower in the sky, and the stars have emerged more brightly visible; a true dusk is settling, and it is becoming increasingly difficult to note where the white of the horizon meets the white of the sky. What this means is that no matter my grandfather's careful calculations, no matter his long preparation, polar night is upon them. "We should be farther along," he says. "I don't know what happened to the days."

"We'll make do," Franklin says, but my grandfather can hear weariness and resignation in his voice. "Blackest night, blackest night, light, light, light," he clucks, and totters off to tell the children.

That evening, a cold and unforgiving storm comes over the ice like an avenging angel and pins them where they are for three weeks.

THEY DO WHAT THEY MUST, given the time of year and the storm: construct a winter depot that will shelter them at the base of the range. While they work, a blizzard wipes clean all visibility. The wind is ferocious and pelting; it stings like needles on exposed skin.

The dogs, restless, begin yipping and yelping in a worrisome way. The children suggest making a more permanent shelter for them, so they can be warm, and happy, and against my grandfather's objections, a vote passes, and the children set about making a second depot. They manage it, but just barely.

The next bout of weather seems to come from the pit of the earth; it announces itself with a howl and circles the ice like punishment from the gods. The temperature drops. The snow pushes against the depot walls in steep drifts.

The children are frightened. There is nothing to say. A mistake has been made; they should be home by now. But whose mistake was it?

"Disaster, starvation, otherworldly endurance, the crumpling of the will, snow blindness, frostbite," Franklin says, later, in their tent. "I can feel it all coming."

"I know," my grandfather says. "I can feel it too." He reaches for his penguin friend and gives his sloping shoulder a gentle squeeze. "This climate is unbearably cruel. There's nothing we could've done." He takes a long drink of brandy, then another. The lamp is lowered. My grandfather is exhausted. He can feel his black mood returning.

Outside the depot it is −67 degrees. To not achieve the Pole before the change of the season is devastating to the expedition, but the journey will have to be halted. A small mercy: that evening, the wind abates, quiets, abandons them completely.

COOPED UP, THE CHILDREN MOPE, circle, they exclude. They're listless and fatalistic. No stories get through to them. No calls for a stiff upper lip, no tales of endurance ring true, they've turned inward. There are no songs that Franklin can sing to get them roused to the clean and clear schedule that must be kept during these long and disciplined and dark days.

They will not wash. They refuse to exercise. "Your toes will blacken and fall off!" Franklin pleads with them. "Cuts on fingers will infect and transform into brain-frying fevers. We will have to amputate your feet if you don't move!" This gets the children to shuffle around the depot, but they make faces the entire time. In the mornings, they slink from one corner to the next. In the evenings, they sing a song they've made up called "Oh the Tedium, Oh the Monotony, the Betrayal Has Been Great."

What's the matter with you children? my grandfather would like to scream. *I'm the one who's sick.* He stands. He opens his mouth to say something but decides against it. Hjalmar sits with his head in his hands, eager for all of this to be over. The children say nothing. They set their little faces in angry scowls.

In one of their evening plays, a large polar bear swims across the North Sea to lay waste to an unsuspecting village. In another, a heavy cloud rains a wall of knives. "Every awful thing that has happened is your fault," the children say to my grandfather. He closes his eyes and pretends not to hear. It hasn't escaped his notice that Hjalmar isn't participating in these productions, and when they get to the final play of the night he understands why. This one is called "Hjalmar's Lament." It's the story of a young boy, who has neither mother nor father, asking everyone he meets for help. He is forsaken, and shivers; he is the lowest of the low. Finally, a baker sets upon him with a rolling pin and leaves him beaten in the street.

MONTHS PASS. Outside the depot's door, the night is thick and unending, black with no texture, the absence of light.

"We'd hoped to avoid this," Franklin says. "How we had hoped."

The food they've brought with them is dwindling, and what hasn't spoiled already will certainly do so soon. Everyone is hungry. Their supplies will not make it to spring. The children talk of soaking their harness straps until the leather is soft enough to eat; they consider their boots, their socks.

Franklin is unhappy and quiet, because he knows what happens next. My grandfather is saddened by the prospect, for he has become fond of the dogs as well.

"Someone has to do it," Franklin whispers when everyone is pretending to sleep. "It's why we brought them in the first place."

No one will help him. No one will even hand my grandfather a knife. He sets off with creaky bones for the second depot and returns with enough gamey meat to last another month if rationed correctly. The children are silent and unforgiving. They eat the meat. They cough and cry, but not a single child refuses. *The difficult is what takes a little time*, thinks my grandfather. They avoid eye contact and sleep as far away from him as possible.

"You can't feel badly at this point," Franklin whispers.

My grandfather doesn't answer. He is looking darkly at the ceiling. Those dogs were the sweetest creatures, so easy to love. They licked his hand; they had no complaints. So much of his life has been spent heading in a single direction, and it's brought him here. He can feel his own brain dimming. Where is he going? What is it he sees? With a cough he returns.

"I said, they're angry, but it's not your fault," murmurs Franklin. He sees there is blood on my grandfather's chin. Delicately, as though handling a child, he dabs it off. He notices that my grandfather is avoiding looking at something in the southern corner of the depot but cannot see or imagine what it might be.

A STILLNESS—A COLLECTIVE FUGUE—settles over the group. Within another month Franklin is amputating frostbitten feet and hands. The bandaged children hop around, confused and furious. Their songs lose their melody, become deep guttural chants. After my grandfather lowers the lamp each night, there is a shush of masturbation that comes from the heap of sleeping bags before each child falls into troubled dreams.

The expedition turns its corner. The children lash out at one another; they become cruel. They catalog the faillings of their friends, of Franklin, of my grandfather. They've taken to taunting the remaining dogs.

Why is this happening to us? Why did you bring us here? Why did you do this to us? Why? the children cry out. My grandfather knows they will wait forever for an answer. But soon they quiet; they stop asking and my grandfather is too tired to give the question the consideration it deserves.

"THEY'RE GETTING OLDER," Franklin says one night as he and my grandfather are walking the perimeter of their camp. They are taking measurements of the ice. "They're not quite themselves."

"It's not just that," my grandfather says. His energy has left him, his throat is raw. His stinging eyes won't stop watering. It's all he can do to stay standing on the ice, to not lay his head down and go to sleep. "They are terrible children. They're plucking your feathers while you sleep."

"I know," says Franklin, rubbing his back.

Above them, the dark sky is pricked with starlight. It unfurls like a sail and covers them completely. It feels as though they have truly found the end of the world. "It's beautiful," Franklin says. As they watch, a curtain of light, green and blue, is drawn across the southern sky. It shimmers, and bends; it points to some larger mystery; it moves as though responding to music neither of them can hear. To the questions of why one leaves the comfort of home to traverse such an inhospitable landscape, one answer might be this, the very thing they are witnessing.

"At moments such as these," my grandfather says, reciting from memory, "a man may feel as though he is at the bottom of some great and deep ocean, gazing up through the depths to the peaceful surface and the silent, folding waves." He coughs. "Let's just stay here a little longer."

Franklin, looking up, can think of nothing to say.

WHEN THEY GET BACK to the depot, the door is tied shut from the outside. Inside, they see only Hjalmar. He's sitting near the stove, with his knees pulled to his chest, crying softly into his elbow. "They left," he says. "They took the rest of the dogs."

The depot has been emptied. All the sleeping bags are gone. Half the biscuits. Most of the dog meat, one or two maps, though my grandfather with relief sees his navigation bag still hooked above the worktable.

"I wanted to go with them," Hjalmar says. "But they wouldn't let me."

"You should've insisted," my grandfather says. His ears are ringing with heat. He takes off his coat and goes to lie down near the stove. Franklin brings a blanket to cover him. "Oh," he says, when he checks my grandfather's forehead.

My grandfather can feel his pulse pushing all rational thought into small, winding rivers behind his eyes. This fever . . . it's a bright one. Hjalmar begins to fret. He brings my grandfather tea, brings him his book, tries to get him to take some pills that look like raisins. He stands and pulls my grandfather's navigation pouch from the wall and begins listing and cataloging its contents.

"Let him sleep," Franklin says.

"His gums are bleeding," Hjalmar whispers. "I know," is the reply. "It's not good."

Leave me alone, my grandfather thinks. He closes his eyes and tries to send his mind to the back of his skull. *Here's the order of the expedition,* he thinks. *After the mountains, an inland lake. A large bird. A winter depot. A rookery. The pole.*

"We're at the winter depot now," says Hjalmar softly, applying pressure to the bridge of my grandfather's nose.

"Right," my grandfather says. "Of course." He is having trouble feeling his legs. He thinks: *my ship, my dogs, the children.* "They will surely perish," he finally says. The thought brings him no sadness whatsoever.

HIS FEVERED MIND opens its letters. He's back aboard his first ship, a young captain, nervous, waking early to see the ocean, dark blue and leaden and still, achieve its creased texture under a swift-rising sun. He glides like a tern over a crevasse that opens at the base of a volcanic Mount Erebus. Now he is gripping hands with Frederick Jackson, and Frederick is saying *hull, salmon, sledge, good luck, good luck, good luck.*

Darkness. Then, in a large lecture hall, he listens as the speaker at the podium raises his elegant, bearded chin to the quieting crowd. "Our clothing," the man begins, "was made from sealskin, reindeer skin, wolf skin, Burberry cloth, and gabardine. Our sledges carved from Norwegian ash, with steel-shod runners made from American hickory."

Sitting in that great hall, he is filled with admiration and jealousy. He leans forward to hear more, but his mind

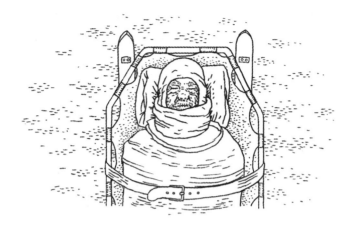

is pinwheeling now and won't cooperate, and suddenly he is home, in Svalbard, it is Christmas, and his older cousin is visiting. They are young, which is why they are sharing his bedroom. His older cousin has removed his pants and is making lewd gestures. My grandfather knows what is coming next, he has never forgotten it. He can hear his parents talking in the next room. They are speaking of his loneliness, his strangeness, and his penchant for solitude and self-pity. *Why is no one helping that boy?* he wonders.

"Yes?" the speaker says.

Every face in the lecture hall turns toward him. There is a deep and resonant silence. But my grandfather has caught himself up. He's seen too late that the speaker has no body. He is only a floating head.

"Not today," my grandfather says. "Forgive the interruption."

When he wakes, it is evident to him that some time has

passed. He can't move his head. Above him he sees a scud-
ding cloud. Things smell white and clean, and he can hear
the crunch of footsteps on snow. It's bright, and he must
close his eyes to the streaming sun. "How long have I been
sick?" he asks. Franklin and Hjalmar, who are pulling the
sledge that my grandfather is strapped to, almost fall over
from surprise at the sound of his voice.

"Two months almost!" Hjalmar exclaims. "I can't believe it."

"A miracle," says Franklin. They've both got their harnesses off and are peering down at my grandfather, who is
trying to stand.

"Franklin wouldn't leave your side," says Hjalmar.
"He just sat there, feeding you apples and blueberries all
mashed up."

"You would've done the same," Franklin says.

Hjalmar tells him they're fifty nautical miles away from
the pole, and that they've already passed Mount Helmer
Hanssen. They'd already spotted, in the distance, the
children who had peeled off from their expedition with
the dogs.

"All dead," says Hjalmar, sadly.

"What about the rookery?" my grandfather asks.

Franklin tears up. "Gone, gone," he says, picking up
his harness. "It's not how I remember." Hjalmar adjusts
his hood. "We kept walking. There was nothing else to be
done. We should go and set up the tent."

"I'd like to see," my grandfather says, and, working together, they unclasp his restraints, unzip his blanket, and
prop him up on the sledge. The ice stretches and bends

to the horizon. It's reflective: in it he can see the quick-forming clouds. To the north stretches the Queen Maude Range, and beyond that the barrier ice, and beyond that his ship. What else, what else? He's too tired now to keep his eyes open. But they see, they see . . . he doesn't know what it is, at first. "Franklin," he says, and reaches for the binoculars, and raises them. Settled, sighted, a round view, and he sees it's one of the dogs, bounding happily toward their small group across the ice. He approaches with his black tongue hanging out, panting loudly in the cold air. His eyes are like beautiful blue marbles. The snow has begun to flour his fur. "Where are your brothers?" my grandfather says. "And where is your sister?"

"Right here," says the dog. And then Franklin disappears, and then Hjalmar, and the world is without color, and then without any sound. When he wakes again, there are flowers on the windowsill. And when he wakes again, they are gone.

FAMILY, HAPPINESS
\\\\\\\\\

THE MAN AND WOMAN were younger then, and one
morning they sat together by the pond. Between them, on
a towel, was the baby, a boy. The plan had been to take
him swimming. But for now, he lay on his back, between
them, while they discussed other things. He was their
child, but that's not how it felt to the man. It was more like
he wasn't not theirs.

The man held out his finger and waved it in front of
the baby's face. The baby's small hand reached up and
grabbed it. Did you see that? the man said. He brought it
right to his mouth.

He does that, the woman said. She held her head in her
hands and didn't look.

Right to his mouth! the man said. I think he's hungry.

No, the woman said. He just does that.

They had both dreamed of this morning, and here it was.

IT WAS MID-SUMMER. They'd been told no one else would be at the pond, and that was indeed how things had turned out. In fact, they hadn't seen anyone else for days, since this was the vacation they'd planned. They'd parked and walked a quarter mile from the road through the forest before the pond became visible.

What was happening was the baby wasn't taking the breast. All night he screamed and screamed.

Now he seemed content, however, to be on his back on the blanket.

Happy to watch the low clouds shift slowly above him.

I'M ALONE HERE, the woman said. I feel alone. And I shouldn't be.

I know, the man said.

He pushed his palms together.

We will never be done with this, she said.

This! he wanted to say. But he knew what she meant.

His eyes were burning. He felt like he hadn't slept in years.

But he also knew that whatever he was feeling, she was feeling worse.

EVENTUALLY THE SUN BROKE THROUGH the clouds. In the distance, the light became like solid columns connecting the land and sky. God's fingers, her mother had called them. Focus, she'd said when they appeared, and the woman said the same thing now, quietly, *focus*. She stood and shucked her shorts.

She gingerly pulled her shirt over her head. Her nipples were cracked and angry.

Maybe this pond isn't good for swimming, the man said.

But she was looking off into the near distance and didn't answer.

The baby had found his feet and clung to them.

That's new, the man said.

She reached for the baby and brought him to her.

Do you want me to come? the man said.

No, she said.

Do you want me to take a picture? he said. But she didn't answer.

THE POND WAS THICKLY RINGED by tall grass. The water dark and still. She was nude and held the baby gently in front of her. There was no one but the man to see them as she walked slowly over the grass to the edge of the water.

She held him away from her own body as though he were himself coming apart.

The man knew he should be walking with her, to the pond. But he also knew it was something he did not want to do. He reached for the camera then put it down. He'd become angry and was waiting for someone to notice.

Husband and wife, he was thinking. Mother and father.

ALL OF THE GRANDPARENTS were dead and none of them had met the baby. None could offer help. But they did walk as ghosts. Sometimes they were welcomed, and sometimes they were shunned.

Try harder, one of them had said in the nursery. It should be beautiful, and easy.

Shhhhhh, another had said.

SHE HELD THE BABY by his arms now and dipped his feet in the water. He let out a small cry. She lowered him further, up to his chubby knees, and he calmed. She waded deeper, to her own knees, to her waist, to her chest, where she held the baby and the forest went silent.

The baby had a look on his face that said, this is interesting.

Suddenly a small red bird landed on the pond's bank. Little one, little one, what do you see? he sang.

NO ONE MOVED. FINALLY, the baby, their baby, now submerged up to his small concave chest, opened his mouth and began to answer. The sound was like a gathering of wind, a language now forming and wholly his. The day stopped. The columns of light held their shape. The pond grew large and the water clear. They had all the time in the world. There was no pleasure as pure as the sensation at hand, no pleasure as sweet as being held by his mother and watched by his father, and the sound he made moved toward them and through them until they understood that it filled the clearing and had come from themselves.

Little one, little one, what do you see? the bird called again.

And they waited for an echo.

THE DIVER
\\\\\\\\\

ONE MORE, ONE MORE. And let's begin like this: first there was an earthquake; then there came a giant wave . . . but of the wave itself, the boys heard and remembered nothing. They'd been asleep, and when they woke and looked out their bedroom window, they saw their world had filled with water. It seemed impossible that the sea had risen this far inland, but that's the way it was. The water was dark and sludgy, thick with debris. It had moved through their neighborhood in the middle of the night like some slow, obscure beast who'd unhinged its jaw and quietly swallowed up everything they had ever known.

They climbed up to the attic and scrambled onto the

roof of their house. Still water stretched everywhere, as far as they could see. Most of the houses in their neighborhood were nearly submerged, their windows dark. Everything was deserted, everyone gone. They heard no sirens. No parents called for their children. A tremendous quiet lay over the land. Night fell. In the distance, they saw fires push orange heat into the dark sky. Where were *their* parents? The boys didn't know.

On the second day, they watched a flotilla of fire ants blanket by. On the third day, the sky filled with silent birds. On the fourth day, they woke to find an empty canoe turning in slow circles just outside their window, and they lowered themselves down and climbed in. They paddled through their water-sunk streets calling for their friends. They called the names of their parents and teachers and coaches, but no one replied.

Why had this happened? And why to them? At first, they were sad, but then, with great effort, they stopped feeling that way. The world was new, that was the only way to look at it.

Mornings, they ate quietly in the attic before mapping out their days. They paddled farther and farther from their home. When the sun went down, it felt as though they were floating through a dark, flooded cave; the only sound that came to them was the kiss of their paddles stirring the water. Every so often an unusual ripple pushed toward the canoe, or they heard a shallow splash as if a fish had jumped, giving them the distinct feeling they were being watched and followed. But each time they turned toward the sound they saw only their own flat wake licking eerily away from them.

Every night, they returned to the attic, climbed into their shared bed, and listened to the quiet world outside until they fell asleep. They didn't want to be alone, but clearly were; the town was flooded, everyone had forgotten about them. And they knew that the sooner they accepted that, the happier they'd be.

"BUT OF COURSE they hadn't been forgotten," Soren said, and held up his hands. His two boys sat still in their beds. They had complained about putting on their pajamas, and brushing their teeth, how it was dark outside but not *that* dark, but now, in the yellow lamp light of their shared bedroom, they'd gone quiet with anticipation. "And they *were* being watched," Soren continued. "For the splashes they heard while they were paddling came from Old Gr'mer. He'd come in on the wave and was, in many ways, responsible for it."

Soren shifted his weight at the foot of the younger boy's bed as they leaned closer. The boys hated to hear about Old Gr'mer, but they loved him too. He'd come to them in a dream, and as far as Soren could tell from the pictures they'd drawn and shown him, he was some sort of red squid the size of a bus. His black beak chomped relentlessly even when he was not eating. He was evil, shifty, a plain fact of the world; but he was also lonely in the deep, and so with his many tentacles, he held the souls of drowned people to keep him company in the abyssal plain he called home. But now and then he rode in on tsunami waves, which was something the boys had been learning about in school. Where they'd gotten the idea of a soul collector, Soren had no idea.

"But don't worry," Soren added. "They don't encounter him yet. Because that was the night, when they were about to give up, that they met the Diver."

"Did they see his light?" the younger boy asked.

"It hung in front of him like a large blue lantern," Soren said, "and glowed in the depths as he made his way up their street. They watched from their attic window. It was unmistakable. He looked like an angler fish. They knew, immediately, they were no longer alone, and that was something to celebrate."

HANA WOULDN'T TELL Diver stories anymore. She thought they were too violent and sad. Soren could hear her now from the bedroom; she was on the phone in the kitchen. She'd spent the day canvassing, which always left her a little depressed. People listened, nodded, said, I know, *I know*, but no one signed at the door, no one donated money. I'm not asking for much, she'd say. Vote the right people in! Don't let the planet choke! When she was tired, she'd yell at the boys for leaving lights on when they weren't in the room, or for wasting water as they brushed their teeth.

"Right, right," Soren heard her say. Her sister, Chloe, was going through a bitter divorce—that was who Hana was talking to—and she thought nothing of calling late to keep Hana on the phone for hours while Soren put the boys to bed. After these long conversations, Hana would hang up and come to bed glassy-eyed and defeated. Who *isn't* depressed? she would say, and fall into a restless sleep. Who isn't dispirited by the way things are going? Who isn't unhappy?

Because their lives were busy and stressful, full-time jobs, two growing kids, and because his own mild depression had returned, and because a feeling of helplessness about the state of the deteriorating world had numbed them into their own private corners, Soren both knew what she was talking about and had no idea what she was talking about all at once.

"CAREFULLY," SOREN CONTINUED, "the Diver opened the front door to their house, and they heard him walk upstairs. Then, his brass helmet lifted through the surface of the water, and, with seagrass coming off of him in cold, green strings, he stepped into the attic.

"For a long time, he just stood there, dripping water, like he was some sort of ghost himself. He was taller than the boys had expected. But they knew it was him: iron shoes, brass helmet with four port lights, heavy gloves. There was something unusual about his appearance, however. His helmet was streaked and dented, not shiny but a dull, greenish color. It had long ago rusted to his corselet and could not be removed. His canvas diving suit was stained yellow. Barnacles had colonized his gloves. He looked very old, as if being in the water for all these years had finally caught up with him. This came as a bit of a shock to the boys, who had always imagined him to be a young man. While they couldn't see his face through the helmet's forelight, they could hear his breathing, and now he grew quiet. Finally, in a low, deep, patient voice, he explained what he was doing there.

"As everyone knew, he followed Old Gr'mer and worked to free the souls he held in his pulsing grip," Soren went on. "But this last wave had been so large, and Old Gr'mer, in his loneliness and fury, had grown so powerful that even he was having trouble keeping up. *I am old*, he said, *and tired. Still, this is important work, and I need your help.* What he meant by this wasn't exactly clear to the boys. But it would be soon."

Soren heard Hana open and shut the refrigerator door and listened for her footsteps down the hall. The last time Chloe had called, Hana had told her: you have to stay attached to life somehow. Soren could've told her how that would be received. Why don't *you* get a divorce, blow your own life up, and *then* tell me how I should feel? Chloe had said and hung up. He waited now for a sound from outside the boys' room but heard nothing.

"Anyway," he said. "Where was I?"

NEXT MORNING, THE DIVER woke them gently and presented each of them with a small, collapsible bathyscope, through which they could watch from the surface as he went about his underwater work. The boys tied them around their necks like binoculars. Once they left the attic, the Diver sat in the front of the canoe with his back to the boys, whispering directions as they quietly paddled across the blackish water. They passed a gas station, an antique store, a train-car diner. The tops of pine trees pushed through the water and stretched their dark and resting arms in ominous welcome. Eventually, the Diver held up a closed fist—meaning stop—and stood. Around his old, dented helmet a halo of blue electricity began to fritz and snap like a mosquito trap. He made a slight nod in their direction, indicated that they should use the bathyscopes he'd made, crossed his arms over his chest, and tipped over the side. Water swallowed him up.

From the canoe, the boys watched his blue lantern glide through the murk. Then, peering through their bathyscopes, they saw he'd landed in the middle of a street—flooded cars lined the empty block, and large branches, which had been swept a great distance by the rushing water, now lay still on the sidewalk. They saw no people. How strange it was to see this neighborhood underwater, and so clearly; it was like peering into an empty aquarium. Now, the Diver's light seemed to grow in strength, and with horror they saw the bodies of people who had been drowned by the wave strewn everywhere. Most had kelp caught in their hair, and many were without clothing; some had gaping, bloodless wounds. All were ghostly in the blue light of the Diver's lantern.

Wrapped around the torso of each was a dark red tentacle, which tethered each floating body to the ground.

The Diver moved gracefully; he was slow and deliberate. When he reached the first body, an old man, the Diver took his drifting hand and gently lifted his arm; he unsheathed his knife, then, with care, slid the blade under the tentacle wrapped around the man's ribs. It was difficult, sawing work—and with every cut and plunge of the Diver's knife, the water became cloudy with jets of pus and decay.

Once severed, the tentacle released its grip and fell to the Diver's feet. For a minute, the old man remained suspended in the water, arms extended over his head as though stretching at the end of a very long nap. Then he stiffened, brought his hands to his face, and disappeared into a cone of golden, pulsing light. The boys looked away from their bathyscopes as this light lifted up and out of the water near their canoe, held its circular shape, then, with a sound like a thunderclap, disappeared. Then all was quiet, the Diver alone again in the putrid water as he made his way to the next tethered soul.

"THEY CONTINUED THIS WORK for hours," Soren said, "with the boys on the surface, in their canoe, watching and marking off their map every time the Diver cleared an area of drowned souls. They were making progress, for sure. But there was something else the Diver had told them: the more souls they discovered and cut loose, the angrier Old Gr'mer became. This often led to brutal, repetitive attacks on the Diver as he went about his work. One minute, he would be walking heavily across the seafloor as normal. The next, he would be set upon by angry tentacles—they wrapped around his ankles and wrists, tightened, and pulled—and he would be torn limb from limb."

"No," said the younger boy.

Soren took a sip of water. "It was awful, truly it was. It was a horrible shock to see the Diver ripped apart, and they hadn't believed it would happen. But sure enough, near the end of the day, the Diver found himself overpowered by Old Gr'mer's tentacles, and in terror they watched as he was torn at the joints—his arms and legs scattered while his torso and head were severed—and his pieces, flung widely, floated to the ground."

"That's gross," the older boy said.

"The boys *wanted* to cry out," Soren continued, "but kept quiet, for this is how they were supposed to be of help to him. Once everything had cleared—the tentacles no longer writhing and kicking up silt, the Diver's lantern still emitting its blue light to guide them—they dove from their boat to gather his parts. It was exhausting, but the tentacles didn't recognize them as any sort of threat and left them alone to collect their friend."

Hana walked down the hall past the boys' room. She held the phone against her ear—Soren could tell by her tight shoulders she was upset—but when she saw they were watching, she flashed a thin smile and waved at the boys.

"I forgot she was here for a second," the older boy said.

"What?" Soren said. "Where would she have gone?"

She gave them a thumbs-up, then turned and walked to the kitchen. There was a long silence, in which, for reasons he did not understand, Soren felt a deep chill. "Do you think she saw all the bags?" the younger boy asked.

He was talking about the Ziplocs they'd washed and hung to dry before she'd come home. "I'm sure she did," Soren said.

All three kept their eyes on the doorway as though Hana might return any minute to congratulate them. But she didn't, so Soren began again.

BACK IN THEIR NEIGHBORHOOD, the water was black and still. On the attic floor the boys arranged the Diver's arms and legs and helmet in the shape of a man, as he'd told them to do. They watched for hours, but nothing changed—his various parts just lay there like an empty suit. They zipped their sleeping bags together, to stay close as they slept. But they couldn't sleep, having no idea what would happen next.

He revived as dawn broke. Slowly, his arms scooted closer to his torso, then his legs. Blue light flickered from his helmet, and it too reattached. Then, with a sound like a great exhalation of air, the Diver sat up. He said nothing at first—methodically he moved each arm, his hand, his fingers; he stood and walked around the attic like a rusty old machine. He was certainly the worse for wear, but it was him. *Thank you,* he finally said. The boys were immensely relieved.

From then on, each day they set out according to a grid the boys had drawn of the town. The Diver plunged into the depths, the boys guiding him, and they watched as he released the souls of the drowned. Each man, woman, or child they freed at first stiffened like the old man, then became a blinding, golden light, lifted out of the water, and was seen no more. Sometimes the tentacles attacked, sometimes they didn't. It was no longer shocking. If the boys had to swim after pieces of the Diver, they didn't mind. In fact, it made them feel useful, like they were working at a job only they could do.

But as the days passed, the boys began to notice that with each excursion the Diver was growing more sluggish in his movements, less nimble, clumsy with his knife; he strode across the seafloor with less purpose, as though resigned to the monotony of his difficult work. His blue light began to dim, flicker, and only truly shine for a few minutes at a time. He'd started to repeat himself, when he spoke at all. If they didn't tell him where to go, occasionally he would just stand under the water, still as a statue, as though puzzling through a serious problem in his mind. In the evening, when they'd returned to the attic, he'd slump in the corner and power down as if some old clock in his chest had become weary of keeping time. He never slept, exactly—his feet, in iron shoes, would kick and his arms swatted at things neither boy could see. If they spoke to him, he would not answer.

One night, after he'd been still for a long time, the boys crept across the attic to get a closer look. They saw his canvas suit had frayed at the elbows, his dull knife appeared rusty and caked in tentacle gore. The rotten smell he'd begun to give off was intense, and they held their noses as they climbed over his legs. Careful not to disturb him, they stood on their toes and peered through the forelight in his helmet.

What they saw startled them: the Diver seemed to have no face. Inside his helmet was only a thick, black mist.

What had they expected to see? They didn't know, but it wasn't this. Periodically the mist in his helmet cleared and gave them a glimpse of something like unbounded space—a deep and shapeless darkness pricked with stars. In it, they saw themselves, and the work they had ahead of them. The mist was trying to tell them something. But they had no idea what.

In the morning, the Diver stood slowly and stretched. They exchanged pleasantries, got into the canoe, and went about their work. But the boys had begun to worry, and they wished they'd never looked at all.

"HOW BAD DID IT HURT when he got pulled apart? A lot?"

"I'd imagine so," said Soren. "Pain like you can't really believe. The Diver didn't like getting pulled to pieces, he'd just become used to it. Each time he wearily stitched himself back together, the boys saw little lightning bolts fritzing at the seams of his suit. At the end of each bolt now was tiny blue skull. He didn't talk with the boys about what he was feeling or thinking, though."

The younger boy stirred as though he were about to speak, but his brother put his fingers to his lips. "He can ask a question," Soren said. The younger boy thought for a second, and finally said, "It turns out I don't have a question."

"Can I ask you a question?" Soren said, and pointed to the Band-Aid on his son's nose.

"It makes him feel comfortable," the older boy explained. "He's not hurt. He just wears it."

"I'm okay," the younger boy said.

Soren nodded. "Anyway, while all this was happening, Old Gr'mer had been gathering strength. And he'd grown infuriated. After their last excursion, he'd followed them to the attic, so he knew where they stayed at night." Soren cleared his throat. "And soon, in fact the night after the boys looked into the Diver's helmet, he attacked."

"Were they ready?" asked the younger boy.

"Not at all," said Soren. "He caught them completely by surprise. For a giant squid, he was quite a subtle swimmer. He moved without sound and expanded like a large red stain across the water, changing colors whenever he wanted to. If it was night, there was no chance you'd see him. So it was without any warning that he pulled the roof off the attic and began his battle with the Diver. His tentacles were enormous: each was the size of a barge's anchor line, and every sucker was like a giant pair of closing lips.

"Old Gr'mer squeezed one of his limbs around the Diver and brought him to his gnashing beak, but the Diver plunged his knife deep into the tentacle until it released its hold and he fell to the slick attic floor. The boys were terrified, but the tentacles did not reach for them just yet, and from where they sat huddled in the corner of the attic, they could hear the Diver's heavy breath as he cut and slashed at the attacking squid. They believed in the Diver—even though he was tired, he was doing well—but Old Gr'mer was determined and furious. He hissed and clicked his giant beak as his tentacles slapped the floor trying to hook the Diver's legs, and in the process smashed most of the attic to pieces."

"Their house?" the older boy asked.

Soren nodded. "Destroyed. At that point, though, the house was the last thing on their minds. This battle went on and on. They were fighting for their lives, and the tide seemed to turn on each of them over the course of an hour. Eventually, however, it was clear the Diver had become truly exhausted—and each time Old Gr'mer pulled him closer to his beak it took him longer to free himself. The boys froze. They had no idea what to do. Finally, Old Gr'mer's remaining tentacles worked in tandem; they swept the Diver's legs and, in one smooth, unfurling motion, wrenched him off the floor by his feet. He opened his great black beak and the boys closed their eyes—they knew this was it for the Diver, and probably for them as well. But," Soren said, and coughed, "right at that moment, the Diver must've gotten Old Gr'mer with a lucky stab— because with a high-pitched scream, the mysterious squid fell back into the water around their house and swam away. The attic was destroyed, but they'd survived."

"I have to go to the bathroom," the older boy said, and jumped off the bed. Soren moved his knees to let him by.

In the low light of the bedroom, his younger son hugged, then flattened, then hugged his pillow again. He looked so much like Ilana that people stopped them on the street to comment on it. For this reason, Soren loved him just a little more, though he would never say so. "What's on your mind?" Soren asked.

"Nothing," he said, hesitating.

"We can talk," Soren said. It was late. The traffic sounds outside the window had gone almost completely away.

"Where are their parents?"

"Oh," Soren said. "Right." He clasped his hands together and looked to the window. He'd moved them offstage and really hadn't thought about it, but of course it mattered. "Give me a second," he said. He felt the answer coming, and didn't want to lie, but before he could respond he heard the toilet flush and the older boy returned. "We'll get there," he said. He wiped at his nose. "Now, where was I?"

"Old Gr'mer," the older boy said.

"Right. They'd survived the attack but no longer had a home, which made them sad. The Diver had been listening to what they were saying, and he sympathized. But now was not the time to think about that, he told them. Now was the time to follow Old Gr'mer and finish what they'd started. And so they did. They set out together to bring Old Gr'mer and his horrid quest to an end."

BY CANOE, THE TRIP TOOK most of the morning—they paddled past upturned cars, small rainbow slicks of oil, the occasional fire. They paddled past the fifth floor of an office building whose windows were blown out. The blue corona of light around the Diver's helmet flickered as he trailed one hand over the canoe's side and signaled to the boys by pointing where he wanted to go. They un derstood he was following the squid by reading the water, but how he was doing that remained a mystery. Soon, they saw nothing familiar. The sea had risen again; it was gray and leaden, and stretched in an unbroken line all the way to the horizon. The sunken world was the sunken world, there didn't seem to be anything anyone could do about it.

No birds called. The air was heavy with salt. The Diver held up his hand and the boys stopped paddling. What they heard was a sound not unlike the absence of sound, followed by a distant inhalation. Then a tremendous howling wind ripped across the water. It was Old Gr'mer's doing. He whipped up the waves, and everything became unrecognizable.

"THE FIGHT WAS BRUTAL," Soren said. "Old Gr'mer had lured them to his lair, and in the deep water The Diver was clearly at a disadvantage. Old Gr'mer's lair was right on the edge of a huge, breathing fissure that opened like a jagged mouth in the earth; it sucked up large amounts of water then forcibly spat it out. The boys worried and watched uneasily; through their bathyscopes they saw their tired friend slash and cut and try to stay away from the fissure, while Old Gr'mer reached for him with a seemingly unlimited number of tentacles. It was impossible to say who was winning, and it seemed as though the fight would never end. The water became inky with Old Gr'mer's blood, and the fissure sucked this up like a vacuum and expelled toward the boys. This bloody darkness then blossomed and moved for them like the mist they'd seen inside the Diver's helmet, and soon the water grew so cloudy that the boys couldn't see what was happening at all.

"Meanwhile," Soren continued, "the waves were really

kicking up. The boys abandoned their bathyscopes and lay on their backs in the canoe so they wouldn't tip over. The sky had grown dark, and the low clouds above them were like great, twisting leaves. As they went up one wave and down another, they held hands and closed their eyes—and they pictured the Diver, exhausted, piercing Old Gr'mer's tentacles with his knife. They saw him make slow slashing motions through the heavy water. Then, they imagined his suit coming apart in the blue light of his helmet, imagined him being pulled closer and closer to Old Gr'mer's enormous chomping beak. They were afraid for their friend, afraid for their lives.

"But just as they were beginning to lose all hope, the waves churning around them settled and stopped and they heard a great shushing sound. All at once columns of golden light broke through the surface of the water and lifted toward the night sky.

"Soon, everything was quiet again, and when the water cleared, they looked over the canoe's side. They saw that the battle had in fact been very brutal and had been fought to the last. Old Gr'mer's foul tentacles were scattered everywhere. The fissure had ceased its exhalations. They scanned the seafloor until they saw the Diver's helmet. Though no longer connected to his body, it still gave off its faint blue light and called the boys quietly to their work. Without a word, they stripped down to their underwear, and dove. They found every piece of the Diver except for one of his feet, which must've been swallowed during the battle. They loaded his arms and torso and helmet into the front of their canoe. Each piece was heavy, and it sometimes took both of them to lift it from the water over the side. But eventually they did it. And then they put their shirts back on, turned, and, just as the sun was coming up, began to paddle in the direction of home, though they had no home to return to."

"Was Old Gr'mer gone?" the older boy asked.

Soren nodded. "The Diver had won only by feigning death and allowing himself to be swallowed whole. Once in that squid's rancid stomach, he'd kicked and cut his way out. However, before succumbing, Old Gr'mer had managed one final time to pull the Diver apart—and that's why he was in pieces. After that, Old Gr'mer crumpled into himself as though he were trying to fit somewhere small, and died. The fissure sucked him up."

"Good riddance," the younger boy said.

"My thoughts exactly," said Soren. "And that brings us almost to the end of the story."

THEY DRIFTED AND DRIFTED. Every day, the boys woke with the hope that on the horizon they'd see land, or another boat, or . . . anything at all. But every day, they woke, hungry and thirsty, and saw nothing except brown, waveless water. The days grew infernally hot and the nights were frigid. They waited for the Diver to re-configure himself, but the light was gone from his helmet, and he never did. His canvas suit dried out in the sun and baked until it no longer gave off any smell. After a week of paddling, they understood that the Diver wasn't coming back and that they were all alone. They had no home but their canoe, no idea what would happen next, and that made them afraid.

Then one night, after two aimless weeks on the water, they woke to a sharp buzzing sound. It came from the front of the canoe, where the Diver's parts lay in a heap. The boys held each other as the pieces of his body began to hum and glow with the blue light they thought they'd never see again.

For a long time, they watched the front of the canoe with excitement and caught their breath at every flash of light. But soon it became clear that something was very wrong. For one thing, the Diver's parts would not stitch together. For another, when he finally did talk his voice sounded like it was coming from the bottom of a deep well, and they could not understand a single thing he said. Saddened, they lifted his helmet and placed it on the seat like a lantern. Through the forelight, they could see the mist had returned. His corselet began to glow. They wanted to make sense out of what he was trying to tell them, but they could not—it seemed as though he spoke of things they'd never seen and never would see. But as the night went on, they found they didn't mind so much that they couldn't understand what he was saying. It was reassuring simply to hear his voice again. For hours they listened, and asked questions, and enjoyed being together. They told him what it felt like to be lonely, and what they missed about their old lives. And then in the morning, his light went out for good.

IN THE ROOM, THE BOYS were quiet. "What happened after that?" the younger one finally asked.

"Well," Soren said. "Next day, they saw an island in the

distance, and figured the Diver had somehow led them to it. They began paddling for those dark hills." He wiped his hands on the legs of his pants. He saw that the boys were watching him closely, but he didn't know what else to say. "The world was new. That's all," Soren finally said. "It was theirs to start." In his mind's eye, he saw the island exactly—a steep, volcanic ledge, climbing out of the sea. He saw the canoe heading for it, then the story slipped away.

"Were their parents there?" the younger boy asked.

"Oh," Soren said. "No. Not physically. But they visited them in their dreams. They'd been waiting there. And they missed them so much."

The air in the bedroom felt suddenly thick. Soren could tell that neither boy was satisfied with the story—they sensed when things had gone off the rails and knew when he was just trying to wrap things up—but it was late and he could think of nothing else to say.

"Good night," he finally announced, and stood. He gently pressed the back of his hand to each of their cheeks, walked across the room, and shut the door.

IN THE KITCHEN, Soren poured himself a drink and began to straighten the counter. There wasn't much to do; Hana had gotten there first. Suddenly, he felt as though he might be sick. It quickly passed, but his knees kept the sensation. What had gone wrong? He'd wanted to tell them a story about brothers, one that pushed *against* despair. But why had it pulsed with such loneliness? He rinsed his cup and set it on the rack. As he'd told the story, images of Hana, photos from her childhood he'd seen years ago, had popped into his mind. And then, another old friend, who'd been dead for years. He had no idea why. He swept some crumbs from the toaster into his hand and dumped them into the sink. Then he turned out the lights and stood in the darkness.

He found Hana in their bedroom. She was stretched out and lying perfectly still on the floor. "It's my back," she said. She had her eyes closed to concentrate on the pain. "How'd it go today?" Soren asked.

"Oh, you know. *Knock knock*. Not interested. I must've walked ten miles. Say 'climate' and watch the door close. It's depressing. The world's ending and nobody cares."

Soren took off his shoes and lay down next to her. Through the thin carpet he felt the hard, wooden floor. Hana opened her eyes. "What's the matter?" she asked. "You look like you've seen the ghost of Christmas past."

"No," Soren said. "I'm just thinking about something." She reached over and squeezed his hand. This was the time they had together, and she was ready to talk. But whatever it was he wanted to say kept moving away from him like a silver, glinting fish. He closed his eyes. Relaxing music was playing from Hana's phone on a low volume. He imagined a small, blue light, pulsing. He imagined diving into his wife's body, crawling down her spine, and looking at the painful spot in her back with a powerful underwater lamp.

"It really does feel like the world is ending," he finally said. "But it can't be."

"Well," Hana said. "Let me tell you about an *impor-*

tant election coming up in *your* district . . ." She stretched and sighed.

Their apartment was small, and from his vantage on the floor Soren could see down the dark hallway. From under the boys' bedroom door he saw that one of them had left his bed and was now flicking the light on and off to make his brother laugh.

"Go to sleep," Hana called from the floor, not unkindly. He heard a sharp yelp and scampering and one more stifled laugh. Then they were quiet.

"I hung up on Chloe," Hana finally said. "She called me hypocritical for bringing children into the world. She said it was selfish, and she could see right through it, and see right through my causes, that they amount to zero in the scheme of things and do nothing except make me feel better about myself." Hana sighed. "I've been thinking about this and it's made me feel like I'm orbiting some planet I don't recognize, as though I'm some sort of space rover. I've been distant. I've been cruel. I'm the terrible, busy mother, and the callous, neglectful sister." She squeezed his hand and let go. "But where have you been? Where you've been is no better. When you're angry you stay quiet, but the whole apartment feels it, and you're not happy until everyone is as angry as you."

"That's true," Soren said. "I'm sorry."

"I didn't know what to tell her," Hana said, "because I do think of my children, but they're not the only thing I think about. And I have been selfish: there's so much I want to preserve for them, and one day it's all going to be gone. I love this life. I regret none of it. I just want every-thing to last a little longer."

OUTSIDE, STREETS WERE WET, and the temperature was dropping. Soren closed his eyes. *You would hear the wave*, he thought, *before you saw it*. But was that true? He tried to make his body as still as possible. It was an old trick, and soon he felt the hard surface beneath his shoulders expand to curl around him like a boat. From down the hall, he heard one of the boys leave his bed again and step quietly, cross his room, to find the light switch. On, off, on again. The light flashed under their closed bedroom door like a message from a signal lamp. The story was over. But of course, it would also start again, and maybe this time be different.

"I love you so much," Soren said, and Hana laughed—a sudden bark, hard and full. He reached for her hand, found it. She curled her fingers around his thumb. On the carpet next to them, her phone began to quake and vibrate like a robot's heart.

"Don't pick it up," Soren said.

"I won't," Hana said. She stretched and yawned. Her eyes were closed, too. "I wouldn't dream of it."

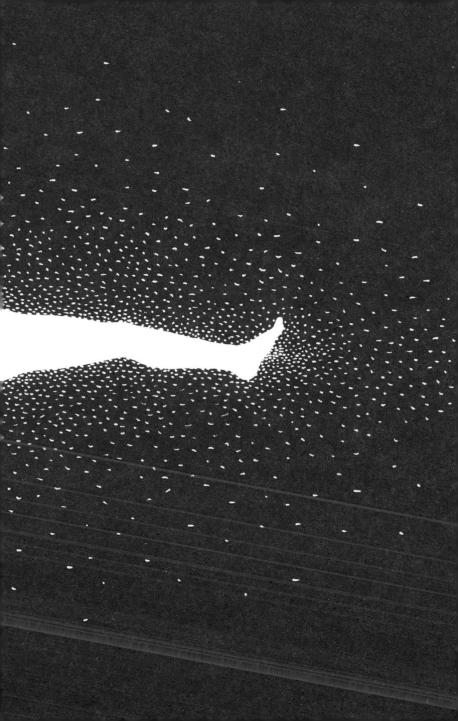

ACKNOWLEDGMENTS

These stories could not have been written without support from the Ucross Foundation and the New York Community Trust, which granted an early version of this manuscript the Ellen Levine Award. That unexpected support during the generative phase of this project was crucial, and meant the world to me. I'd also like to acknowledge and thank the other voices that wandered through these stories as they were being drafted. The poem partially recited in "Fable" is "On Pain" by Kahlil Gibran. In "Holiday," the line "all life exists at the expense of other life" comes from the "The Third Hour of the Night" by Frank Bidart (who is, thankfully, very much alive). That story also owes a debt to the poem "[The day, with all its pain ahead, is yours]," by Derek Walcott.

Thank you to the early readers of these stories for their patience, good cheer, and gentle guidance and to the incredible editors of the various journals where versions of these stories first appeared: Sarah Bilston, Sheila Fisher, Matt Burgess, Paul Yoon, Libby Flores, Raluca Albu, Emma Komlos-Hrobsky, Rob Spillman, Chris Boucher, and Brad Morrow. I'm also grateful for the support and encouragement from colleagues, teachers, family, and friends these last few years: Chloe Wheatley, Ciaran Berry, Clare Rossini, Amity Gaige, Julie Schumacher, Sloane Crosley, Jim Shepard, Charles Baxter, Toby Cox, Nick Manheim, and Calder Gillin. My parents, Dave and Debby Rutherford. Anne Hanley.

With this book I got to work with some of my favorite people in the world: Nayon Cho, Anders Nilsen, Jill Meyers, and Sarah Burnes. What good luck! I feel so fortunate—proud—to have collaborated with such amazing people on this project. Thank you, as well, to everyone at A Strange Object and Deep Vellum.

Finally, to my family: LL & AW, I could not name the boys in these stories, for they would hold no names but yours. This means, of course, that we dreamed them together and they are written for you. Maryhope: again, always, and with love—but deeper and with more miles on the tires this time—thank you.

ABOUT THE AUTHOR

Ethan Rutherford's fiction has appeared in *BOMB*, *Tin House*, *Ploughshares*, *One Story*, *American Short Fiction*, *Post Road*, *Esopus*, *Conjunctions*, and *The Best American Short Stories*. His first book, *The Peripatetic Coffin and Other Stories*, was a finalist for the Los Angeles Times Art Seidenbaum Award for First Fiction, a finalist for the John Leonard Award, received honorable mention for the PEN/Hemingway Award, was a Barnes & Noble Discover Great New Writers selection, and was the winner of a Minnesota Book Award. Born in Seattle, Washington, Rutherford received his MFA in creative writing from the University of Minnesota and now teaches creative writing at Trinity College. He lives in Hartford, Connecticut, with his wife and two children.

223

ABOUT THE ILLUSTRATOR

Anders Nilsen is the author and artist of *Big Questions, Don't Go Where I Can't Follow, Poetry Is Useless,* and several other graphic novels and books of comics in a variety of modes. His work has appeared in *Kramers Ergot,* the *New York Times, Poetry* magazine, *The Believer,* the *New Yorker,* and elsewhere and been translated widely. He is the recipient of three Ignatz awards as well as the Lynd Ward Graphic Novel Prize for *Big Questions.* Nilsen is currently serializing a long-form, full-color graphic novel retelling the myth of Prometheus, set in present-day Central Asia, called *Tongues.* He lives in Los Angeles.

ABOUT A STRANGE OBJECT

Founded in 2012 in Austin, Texas, A Strange Object champions debuts, daring writing, and striking design across all platforms. The press became part of Deep Vellum in 2019, where it carries on its editorial vision via its eponymous imprint. A Strange Object's titles are distributed by Consortium.

Thank you all
for your support.
We do this for you,
and could not do
it without you.

DEEP
VELLUM

Support for this publication has been provided in part by
grants from the National Endowment for the Arts,
the Texas Commission on the Arts, the City of Dallas
Office of Arts and Culture's ArtsActivate program,
and the Moody Fund for the Arts:

PARTNERS

ADDITIONAL DONORS, CONT'D

Cone Johnson
CS Maynard
Daniel J. Hale
Daniela Hurezanu
Danielle Dubrow
Denae Richards
Dori Boone-
Costantino
Ed Nawotka
Elizabeth Gillette
Elizabeth Van Vleck
Erin Kubatzky
Ester & Matt
Harrison

Grace Kenney
Hillary Richards
JJ Italiano
Jeremy Hughes
John Darnielle
Jonathan Legg
Julie Janicke
Muhsmann
Kelly Falconer
Kevin Richardson
Laura Thomson
Lea Courington
Lee Haber
Leigh Ann Pike

Lowell Frye
Maaza Mengiste
Mark Haber
Mary Cline
Max Richie
Maynard Thomson
Michael Reklis
Mike Soto
Mokhtar Ramadan
Nikki & Dennis
Gibson
Patrick Kukucka
Patrick Kutcher

Rev. Elizabeth &
Neil Moseley
Richard Meyer
Sam Simon
Sherry Perry
Skander Halim
Sydneyann Binion
Stephen Harding
Stephen Williamson
Susan Carp
Theater Jones
Tim Perttula
Tony Thomson

SUBSCRIBERS

Andrea Pritcher
Anthony Brown
Audrey Golosky
Aviya Kushner
Barbara Lynch
Ben Fountain
Ben Nichols
Brian Matthew Kim
Carol Trimmer
Caroline West
Charles Dee Mitchell
Charlie Wilcox

Chris Mullikin
Clayton Reed
Courtney Sheedy
Dan Pope
Daniel Kushner
Derek Maine
Elena Rush
Elisabeth Cook
Erin Kubatzky
Eugenie Cha
Hillary Richards
Jason Linden

Joseph Rebella
Kasia Bartoszynska
Kay Engdahl
Kenneth McClain
Kirsten Hanson
Lance Salins
Lance Stack
Lisa Balabanlilar
Margaret Terwey
Martha Gifford
Megan Coker
Michael Binkley

Michael Elliott
Michael Lighty
Michael
Schneiderman
Molly Bassett
Nathan Dize
Ned Russin
Radhika Sharma
Ryan Todd
Shelby Vincent
Stephen Fuller
Stephanie Barr

AVAILABLE NOW FROM DEEP VELLUM

FORTHCOMING FROM DEEP VELLUM

MAGDA CARNECI · *FEM*
translated by Sean Cotter · ROMANIA

MIRCEA CĂRTĂRESCU · *Solenoid*
translated by Sean Cotter · ROMANIA

MATHILDE CLARK · *Lone Star*
translated by Martin Aitken · DENMARK

LOGEN CURE · *Welcome to Midland: Poems* · USA

PETER DIMOCK · *Daybook from Sheep Meadow* · USA

CLAUDIA ULLOA DONOSO · *Little Bird*,
translated by Lily Meyer · PERU/NORWAY

LEYIÂ ERBIL · *A Strange Woman*
translated by Nermin Menemencioğlu · TURKEY

ROSS FARRAR · *Ross Sings Cheree
& the Animated Dark: Poems* · USA

FERNANDA GARCIA LAU · *Out of the Cage*
translated by Will Vanderhyden · ARGENTINA

ANNE GARRÉTA · *In/concrete*
translated by Emma Ramadan · FRANCE

GOETHE · *Faust, Part One*
translated by Zsuzsanna Ozsváth and
Frederick Turner · GERMANY

JUNG YOUNG MOON · *Arriving in a Thick Fog*
translated by Mah Eunji and Jeffrey Karvonen · SOUTH KOREA

DMITRY LIPSKEROV · *The Tool and the Butterflies*
translated by Reilly Costigan-Humes &
Isaac Stackhouse Wheeler · RUSSIA

FISTON MWANZA MUJILA · *The Villain's Dance*, translated
by Roland Glasser · *The River in the Belly: Selected Poems*,
translated by Bret Maney · DEMOCRATIC REPUBLIC OF CONGO

GORAN PETROVIĆ · *At the Lucky Hand, aka The Sixty-Nine Drawers*
translated by Peter Agnone · SERBIA

LUDMILLA PETRUSHEVSKAYA · *Kidnapped: A Crime Story*,
translated by Marian Schwartz · *The New Adventures of
Helen: Magical Tales*, translated by Jane Bugaeva · RUSSIA

JULIE POOLE · *Bright Specimen:
Poems from the Texas Herbarium* · USA

MANON STEFFAN ROS · *The Blue Book of Nebo* · WALES

ETHAN RUTHERFORD · *Farthest South & Other Stories* · USA

MUSTAFA STITOU · *Two Half Faces*
translated by David Colmer · NETHERLANDS

BOB TRAMMELL · *The Origins of the Avant-Garde
in Dallas & Other Stories* · USA